THE YELLOW ROSE OF TEXAS
HER SAGA AND HER SONG

SAN JACINTO MONUMENT, ERECTED IN 1936, ON THE SITE OF THE 1836 BATTLE. COURTESY SAN JACINTO MUSEUM OF HISTORY ASSOCIATION.

The Yellow Rose Of Texas

HER SAGA AND HER SONG

with

THE SANTA ANNA LEGEND

MARTHA ANNE TURNER

Jacket by Don Collins

EAKIN PRESS  Austin, Texas

FIRST EDITION
1986 Printing

Copyright © 1976 By Martha Anne Turner

Published in the United States of America
By Eakin Press, P.O. Box 23066, Austin, Texas 78735

ALL RIGHTS RESERVED. No part of this book may be reproduced in any form without written permission from the publisher, except for brief passages included in a review appearing in a newspaper or magazine.

Library of Congress Cataloging-in-Publication Data

Turner, Martha Anne
    The Yellow Rose of Texas.

    Bibliography: p.
    Includes index.
    1. Folk-songs, American — Texas — History and criticism.
    I. Title.
ML3561.Y44T8   784.4′9764   76-17116
ISBN 0-89015-586-0

INTRODUCTION

MARTHA ANNE TURNER'S book on the Yellow Rose of Texas is as good an example as you will find of grass roots history—something we need more of. Unlike most orthodox historians, who start at the top and deal with great events and important persons, she starts at the bottom and studies what they overlook or undervalue.

Carlyle said truly that history is the essence of innumerable biographies, but they are not always by any means the lives of movers and shakers. Greatness among human beings is always a joint product, and many people most of them unheard of, are needed to make a Mozart or a Lincoln—ancestors, teachers, friends, strangers met at critical times, characters in books or legends. Would Wellington have won the Battle of Waterloo if he had gone into it after a bad breakfast or if his barber had had a bad night? One never knows how much credit for great achievements should go to the cooks and barbers, but one can be sure that a thousand humble men and women contribute to every great event and are behind every great man, contributing to his success in a thousand unacknowledged ways. The problem is to identify these minor figures and give them their due. Not often can it be done, but sometimes a grassroots historian does it and we can turn the spotlight on a Scotsman named John Brown, to whom Queen Victoria listened, or an Emily Morgan, who changed the course of Texas history and helped to make a hero out of Sam Houston.

In *Adam Bede* George Eliot noted that in human affairs, as in a watch, "a small, unnoticeable wheel" is the key to the whole operation. Emily Morgan is that small, unnoticeable wheel. If Martha Anne Turner is right—and so far as I know nobody questions it—the outcome of one of the important battles of the world depended on a servant girl whose unassuming loyalty and self-sacrifice made it possible for Texas to be born.

The grass roots historian looks for such bits of history and treats them with respect. They help us to understand ourselves and our country better. The people themselves paid Emily tribute as they sang about her through the generations. This book will make it hard for formal historians not to do the same.

C. L. Sonnichsen

C.L. SONNICHSEN CHIEF OF PUBLICATIONS
ARIZONA HISTORICAL SOCIETY
EDITOR, JOURNAL OF ARIZONA HISTORY

The Yellow Rose Medallion

EMILY MORGAN, the acknowledged *Yellow Rose of Texas*, was the inspiration for a special edition of a sterling silver and gold medallion minted in 1975 to commemorate her role in Texas' independence.

Designed by Claude T. Riley of Donna, a veteran coin collector and Texas history buff, the medal is cast from a mold hand-sculptured by Casey McCullough of San Antonio. The obverse side of the medallion presents an exquisite full-blown rose in 24-karat gold on a mirrored background with *Yellow Rose of Texas* engraved above.

The reverse side quotes one stanza of the song inspired by the Texas heroine. With pendant ring and chain attached the medallion is mounted in a handsome case and is accompanied by a historic commentary over the author's signature.

The first two coins struck were presented as necklaces to Texas' First Lady, Janey Briscoe, who is herself a Texana enthusiast, and to Martha Anne Turner.

Courtesy TEXAS MEDALLIONS, INC.
BOX 1111, ALAMO, TEXAS

Acknowledgments

FOR their interest and courtesies extended me while this project was in progress, I express my deepest appreciation to the following persons: Dr. Elliott T. Bowers, president; Dr. Donald Stalling, former director, Department of English; Dr. Melvin Mason, professor of English; Dr. Kent Jones, professor of English; Mrs. Josephine Bush, rare books and documents librarian; Paul Culp, interlibrary loan librarian; Diana Paney, reference librarian; Dr. Loyce Adams, professor, business administration, all of Sam Houston State University, Huntsville;

Dr. Ralph W. Steen, former president; Dr. Edwin W. Gaston, Jr., professor of English; Mrs. Gloria Frye, former Special Collections librarian, all of Stephen F. Austin State University, Nacogdoches;

Dr. Chester V. Kielman, archivist-librarian, The University of Texas Library; Dr. Dorman Winfrey, director and librarian of the Texas State Library; and photographer Millicent Huff, Austin;

The Honorable Thomas J. Stovall, Jr., Judge, One Hundred Twenty-Ninth District of Texas, Houston; Dr. John Mayfield, Tyler, Texas, and Bethesda, Maryland; musician and composer David W. Guion, Dallas; Ilanon Moon, Willis; Steele and Julia McDonald, Brownwood; the Reverend and Mrs. Walter N. Langham, Kilgore; Felix and Jewel Gibson, Corsicana; David Lindsey, city editor, *The Huntsville Item*; my secretary, Jeanette Koger, Huntsville; Dr. C. L. Sonnichsen, chief of publications for the Arizona Historical Society, Tucson, Arizona.

Contents

Introduction, by C.L. Sonnichsen vii
Acknowledgments x
Foreword xii
Prologue 1
Santa Anna And The Slave Girl At San Jacinto 5
Manuscript Copy Of The Folksong 41
First Copyright Edition Of The Song 49
A Civil War Marching Song 53
Octavo Edition Of 1906 55
Typescript Variant Of 1930 65
Transcriptions By David W. Guion 67
"The Yellow Rose Of Texas" In World War II 79
Reprint Of The First Edition 85
The Mitch Miller Adaptation 87
Boogie Woogie Transcription Of 1956 93
Postscript 95
The Santa Anna Legend 97
Sam Houston 111
Bibliographic Notes 117
Index 131

Foreword

PERHAPS no other song in the history of music has made a greater bid for immortality than "The Yellow Rose of Texas." In 1976, America's bicentennial year, at the song's one hundred fortieth milestone, the symbol of the yellow rose stands beside that of the Lone Star. Furthermore, Emily Morgan, the maid at San Jacinto who inspired it, has stepped out of a footnote to wear the heroine's crown in Texas history.

Many people have succumbed to the charm of "The Yellow Rose of Texas" and have adopted the flower as an emblem. A former United States senator was the first to use the music to attract voters to his campaign rallies and other political candidates have followed his example. American servicemen have sung the lyrics of "The Yellow Rose of Texas" through three successive wars. A yellow rosebush stands sentinel at the gravesite of the distinguished Texan, former President Lyndon Baines Johnson, near the Pedernales River in the state's famed Hill Country. Three treatments of the "Yellow Rose" theme exist under my byline. *The Yellow Rose of Texas: Her Saga and Her Song*, a completely revised version containing new material, is the fourth to be published under my signature.

My interest in both the history and the song dates back several years. But it was not until June of 1969, when I heard a rollicking German oompah-pah band in a Munich rathskeller play "The Yellow Rose of Texas" with excessive vigor, that I decided to investigate the song. The thought suddenly occurred to me that if the music could have such an exhilarating and pleasurable effect on foreigners, then I, a native Texan, should know more about it. As a result, I prepared a paper titled *The Yellow Rose of Texas: The Story Of A Song*, which I read at the fourteenth annual meeting of the American Studies Association of Texas held on the Texas A&M campus on December 1, 1969. The paper was subsequently published in the *Journàl of the American Studies Association of Texas*, Volume 1, 1970.

That initial essay on the "Yellow Rose" was so well received that I was encouraged to pursue the elusive subject further. After revising the original paper, I submitted the manuscript, together with authentic illustrations, to the press of the University of Texas at El Paso. In 1971 Texas Western Press, as the university's publishing division is known, issued the two editions of *The Yellow Rose of Texas: The Story Of A Song*—one in paperback and one in hardcover—as Monograph No. 31 in its nationally acclaimed and award-winning Southwestern Studies series. Carl Hertzog was director of the press at the time and E. H. Antone, executive editor.

The chief satisfaction I had when the book was published was a wealth of fan mail from virtually all sections of the nation and the privilege of using the volume as a text in a course I was teaching at Sam Houston State University—English 470, Literature of the Southwest. Having borrowed the idea for the course from the late J. Frank Dobie and having been inspired by the late Mody C. Boatright's enthusiasm for Southwestiana, I introduced Literature of the Southwest to the Sam Houston campus and was its sole instructor for more than two decades.

Persons of varied tastes—students both young and middle-aged, including faculty wives and professional people—enrolled in Literature of the Southwest. To work with these fine people, who typified a cross section of Texas, has been one of the most gratifying experiences of my career. It is my sincerest wish that *The Yellow Rose of Texas: Her Saga And Her Song* may stand as a memorial to those students, some of whom have hung up their lariats for the last time.

It is, therefore, with the deepest affection and appreciation that I inscribe this volume to all of you who came into my corral, who lit with me the campfires along the trail, as together we saluted an American tradition of strength and courage.

MARTHA ANNE TURNER
MAY, 1976

Prologue

FOLKSONGS are perpetuated in oral tradition and develop variants through transmission from one generation to another. The genre is essentially distinguished from non-folksongs by qualities of fluidity of form and content.[1] The singer of the folksong gives it authenticity as he transmits it. Evidence of the folksong's distinction is notable in contrast with the other basic categories of songs—art songs and popular songs.

Art songs are transmitted from printed scores precisely as their composers wrote them. Popular songs are also transferred through the medium of the printed page in addition to commercial recordings and public exposure. Both basic categories of song are, therefore, somewhat limiting, as their performers are expected to render them according to conventions of music and techniques employed by the composer. Generally much more stereotyped, popular songs may also be sung in keeping with a current musical trend. Or they may be arranged to complement the singer's individual style. Usually they are enormously popular for a time and then suddenly vanish from public fancy as other lyrics as transitory replace them.

Folksongs, as a group, are even more widely accepted than either of the two basic categories. Unlike art songs and popular songs, they circulate for generations and transcend national boundary lines in their appeal to all classes of people. Despite the fact that folksongs are normally perpetuated in oral tradition, they may originate elsewhere.[2] As a matter of record, a song belonging to any one of the three groups may be converted into one of the other two types. Even though folksongs are more widely accepted than the other two, they are frequently converted into one of the basic categories.[3]

"The Yellow Rose of Texas," which originated as a Negro folksong and is now classified as a popular standard, is an example of such a conversion. While oral transmission of the old Negro folksong continued to be heard in various parts of the world, modern musicians have produced a multiplicity of redactions. Notably among these are two which exemplify the basic types. These are the classic transcription for concert artists released by composer David W. Guion in the 1930s and the version attributed to musical arranger Don George and popularized by the television personality Mitch Miller.

All variants of "The Yellow Rose of Texas," as a folksong, attest to its resistance to change.[4] Furthermore, even though the lyrics of the original version have undergone a steady transition since its inception in the nineteenth century, some members of the present generation who heard it for the first time were probably unaware of its genesis and long history. For instance, "A lot of people think Mitch Miller wrote 'The Yellow Rose of Texas.' Others believe Ralph Yarborough did. Both groups are wrong even though Miller's sing-along chorus did make a popular recording of Don George's 1955 version of the song and even though Senator Yarborough has used it often for a campaign song in Texas. The Miller and Yarborough theorists, however, should not be faulted too much for this—misconceptions about the origin of the song have surfaced often during the past century and more."[5]

Even so, the folksong that fought for survival and enriched other musical genre had that special quality lacking in similar melodies, long since forgotten—that intangible something that inspired the world to sing.

Sam Houston

CHAPTER ONE

Santa Anna And The Slave Girl At San Jacinto

AN old legend insists that on each recurring April 21, the anniversary of the Battle of San Jacinto, the specter of a golden-skinned girl resembling a Latin goddess[1] returns to Texas from the East to preside at the famous battlesite. The ghost is that of the long-haired, twenty-year-old mulatto slave girl, Emily Morgan—"The Yellow Rose of Texas"—whose role in the quarters of General Antonio López de Santa Anna y Perez de Lebron at San Jacinto is approaching international legend.[2] Stripped of all illusion the comely mulatto occupies her rightful—but long disputed—place in history as the heroine of the Texas Revolution.

Exceptionally intelligent,[3] as well as beautiful, Emily was an indentured servant and member of the household of Colonel James Morgan, who had brought her from New York to Texas in 1835.[4] When Santa Anna captured the girl at Morgan's Point, at the mouth of the San Jacinto River, her master was stationed at Galveston guarding Texas refugees and the fugitive government officials. Colonel

Morgan, who served as commandant of Galveston from March 30, 1836, to April 1, 1837, had erected the fortification on the island at his own expense.[5] A staunch patriot, the wealthy Morgan had also contributed the use of his ships to the Texas cause and supplied the government with provisions.[6]

As early as 1830 Morgan, a native of Philadelphia, had visited Texas. Impressed with the country's potential, he decided to establish a mercantile business in the Mexican province as the nucleus for a colony. Accordingly, he moved his wife, their son, and two daughters to Texas[7] and, to circumvent the law prohibiting slavery in the province, converted his sixteen slaves into indentured servants for ninety-nine years.[8] Morgan became the agent for Lorenzo de Zavala and several New York financiers who planned to develop land in Texas.[9] In the company's interest he invested in an immense quantity of real estate in the Mexican territory including the point that later bore his name. After laying out the town, Morgan named it New Washington. In 1835, to increase the colony's population, the colonizer brought in a number of Scotch highlanders, free blacks from Bermuda, and other indentured servants from New York. Emily Morgan was said to have been among the latter.[10] Although the girl's name was Emily D. West,[11] she adopted the name of her master and benefactor in conformity with nineteenth-century custom.

At forty-two Santa Anna prided himself on his connoisseurship of women and his reputation as a ladies' man. His arrogance, lust for power, and handsome looks made him exceedingly attractive to women. A man of fastidious tastes with a penchant for expensive attire, Santa Anna was likewise addicted to such luxuries as silk sheets, exquisite crystal stemware, silver serving dishes, and a mounted sterling chamberpot.[12] When Santa Anna invaded Texas at the head of his Mexican troops, he brought with him an octagonal-shaped, three-room, carpeted silk marquee to serve as headquarters. Furthermore, the Mexican general shared his love of luxury with his mistresses. It was said that he had settled lavish estates upon some of them.

The self-styled "Napoleon of the West" was a prestigious figure at the height of his career in 1836. Santa Anna's rise to power had been both cataclysmic and rapid. From a minor officer in the royalist army of Spain in 1821, he advanced to the rank of five-star general, then in 1833, to emperor of Mexico. When Stephen F. Austin was establishing his colony, Santa Anna, at twenty-six, had already racked up a score of better than ten years of military service in some of the most brutal and bloody conflicts with assorted Indians and rebels on record. As an officer of the colonial army of the king of Spain, he was sent to deal with the mobilizing patriots supporting Augustín de Iturbide. When the rebels invited him to join them, his answer was almost wholesale slaughter. Then at two o'clock on the day of the victory he defected to the side of the rebellion. His terms were a promotion to full rank. Prior to this about-face, however, he reported his victory—for whatever it was worth—to his loyalist superiors. Word came back that his reward was a lieutenant colonelcy. He made the revolutionists bid higher for his services. Finally, "at the end of a series of additional revolutions and deft betrayals of everybody who gave him the chance, Santa Anna eventually emerged as a full general and a five-alarm national hero."[13]

Assuming the presidency of Mexico in 1833, Santa Anna immediately set in motion his centralist policies of dictatorship. By January of 1835 all of the Mexican states except Zacatecas and Coahuila-Texas had been crushed under his totalitarian yoke.[14] In 1836 there remained only Texas to subdue.

Near the environs of Harrisburg on April 15, 1836, the main body of the Mexican army had tarried to wait for stragglers. Santa Anna, accompanied by an adjutant and fifteen dragoons, had walked a mile to the town. There they captured two Americans from whom they extracted the information that the Texas government officials had left the morning before for Galveston Island.[15] At three o'clock on April 17, after instructing his men to put Harrisburg to the torch, Santa Anna began the march toward New Washington. Meanwhile, on the opposite side of the bayou the Mexicans had discovered some houses containing women's apparel, fine furniture, a magnificent piano, jars of preserves, chocolates, and fruits, all of which they "appropriated for the benefit of his Excellency and his attendants."[16]

A storm delayed the progress of the troops, but Colonel Juan N. Almonte and a detachment arrived at

New Washington on April 17 just as the fleeing government officials were trying to embark for Galveston. Although the officials had been informed of the pursuit of the Mexican army, *ad interim* President David G. Burnet and his wife barely escaped in a rowboat before reaching the steamship moored in the bay when the Mexican cavalry overtook them. The soldiers would have shot the officials had Colonel Almonte not intervened because of the presence of Mrs. Burnet in the skiff.[17]

Santa Anna, with his contingent of 1,000 infantrymen and equipment, arrived at New Washington at noon of April 18.[18] The settlement was deserted except for the soldiers looting it and Morgan's remaining indentured servants. Legend asserts that the Mexican general first observed the graceful movements of the mulatto beauty at the wharf as she was assisting others in loading a flatboat with supplies. As a virtuoso of feminine pulchritude, it did not take the commander long to decide that Emily would be an integral part of the loot.

Not until they had exhausted Morgan's well-stocked warehouses of such desirable commodities as flour, soap, tobacco, sugar, and liquor—and rounded up several beeves—did the Mexicans burn the town and prepare to depart. Santa Anna reserved the destruction of Colonel Morgan's prized orange grove for his personal attention.[19]

On April 19, after sacking and burning New Washington, Santa Anna took the slave girl and a yellow boy named Turner captive. He tried to bribe the youth, a printer's apprentice of above average intelligence, to ascertain the position of Sam Houston for him.[20] Turner was sent with a detail of dragoons to reconnoiter the Texas army's location. But before leaving the general's entourage, he had "learned from a Negro woman that the Texians were encamped near Lynchburg on the bayou."[21] Undoubtedly, the Negro woman was Emily as she was the only one traveling with Santa Anna's troops. Turner, taking advantage of the speed of the animal, escaped Mexican surveillance and on the morning of the twentieth warned Houston of Santa Anna's approach.[22] Thus Emily Morgan, loyal to the Texans, conveyed her warning indirectly to Houston before she reached the battlesite herself.

It was not until eight o'clock on the morning of April 20, when the Mexicans were ready to move out, that Santa Anna received news of Houston's position. In the meantime, to delay the Mexican commander's advance, Turner misled him into thinking that Houston was on the Trinity River with his ragtag and disgruntled little army.[23] Captain Marcos Barragan rushed excitedly into the smoldering ruins of the settlement at the head of forty-six dragoons and shouted that Houston was close on their rear.[24] The news threw the self-styled "Napoleon of the West" into a panic:

> Upon hearing Barragan's report, he (His Excellency) leaped on his horse and galloped off at full speed for the lane, which, being crowded with men and mules (already started for Lynch's

Ferry) did not afford him as prompt an exit as he wished. However, knocking down one, and riding over another, he overcame the obstacles, shouting at the top of his voice, "The enemy are coming! The enemy are coming."[25]

Santa Anna's fear was projected to the troops, and according to Delgado's account, they had given up "all idea of fighting."[26] Nevertheless, Santa Anna escaped through the narrow exit. When he reached the open prairie he placed Delgado in command of the artillery and ordnance. Delgado restored order and directed a search for the enemy. Unsuccessful, the officers decided that Barragan's report had been either an exaggeration or a false alarm.[27] After several slugs of opium had restored Santa Anna's composure, the troops resumed march.

The intelligence that had thrown Santa Anna into a fit of hysteria on the morning of April 20 was inaccurate. Colonel Sidney Sherman of Houston's Second Regiment had gone out with forty horsemen on reconnaissance duty around New Washington. Within two miles of the somnolent little town, Sherman's detail had encountered Captain Barragan and other mounted Santanistas. Barragan had mistaken the scouting party for the whole Texas force. Sherman and his men pursued the dragoons only a short distance, then concealed themselves in the woods to observe Mexican troop movements.[28]

When Santa Anna discovered Emily at New Washington he had been deprived of feminine companionship for two weeks. Emily was a replacement for the "bride" of his mock marriage in San Antonio before the final assault on the Alamo—lovely seventeen-year-old Melchora Iniega Barrera. Santa Anna and his lady had left San Antonio on March 31 in his royal coach drawn by six resplendent white mules and escorted by fifty elegantly uniformed dragoons.[29] His tent and carpeting, huge supply of champagne, his opium cabinet, and crates of fighting cocks—destined for the gambling hobby in which he indulged on expeditions—were transported by a train of pack mules. When the royal contingent reached the Guadalupe River at Gonzales, on April 2, it was impossible to ford the turgid stream with the heavy carriage. As the commander expected to rejoin Melchora in a short time, he sent her the next day in the heavy vehicle with a trunk full of silver under escort to Mexico City. Rumor has it that the girl later bore the dictator a child and still later was legally married to the Mexican sergeant who impersonated a priest to perform the fake marriage ceremony in San Antonio.[30]

It was an established custom, with no stigma attached, that the Mexicans, even the common soldiers, kept campwomen, or *soldaderas*, to cook and forage for them as well as perform conjugal duties. Some of these women were mistaken for men and accidentally killed at San Jacinto. Commissioner-General John Forbes of the Texas army was accused of deliberately killing a Mexican woman of high birth and her soldier companion found hiding in the tall grass after the battle.[31]

Because of the weight of their additional plunder, the heavy ordnance cases, and cumbersome brass twelve-pound field piece, the Mexican army inched across the rutted, boggy Texas marshlands at less than a mile an hour. To reduce their baggage, they were forced to abandon their knapsacks on the outskirts of New Washington. At approximately two o'clock in the afternoon of April 20 the aggregation reached the perimeter of a large wooded area where a few of Houston's pickets were stationed. Houston's main force, which had made camp on the east side of Buffalo Bayou, was completely obscured by trees and undergrowth. Hastily, then, Santa Anna chose a position on the plains of San Jacinto approximately a mile from Houston's and ordered his men to encamp. The worst possible location, the site violated all military rules. Officers of the Mexican general's staff opposed the choice openly, and General Manual Fernández Castrillón criticized the location almost within Santa Anna's hearing. The commander's aide, Colonel Pedro Delgado, was even more vehement in his disapproval:

> We had the enemy on our right, within a wood, at long musket range. Our front, although level, was exposed to the fire of the enemy, who could keep it up with impunity from his sheltered position. Retreat was easy for him on his rear and right, while our own troops had no space for manoeuvering. We had in our rear a small grove, reaching to the bay shore, which extended on our right as far as New Washington. What

ground had we to retreat upon in case of a reversal? From sad experience, I answer—None!³²

If Santa Anna chose the general campsite for his soldiers injudiciously, he selected the spot for himself and Emily to occupy with care. Like a man on his honeymoon, he had the gaudy marquee set up on a rise with a romantic view overlooking San Jacinto Bay.³³

The few Texas soldiers and the two six-pound cannon—the Twin Sisters—Santa Anna saw upon arrival failed to excite admiration. More interested in what awaited him in the red-striped tent, cocky and confident Santa Anna, nevertheless, ordered Delgado to engage the Texans in a skirmish in a grove of trees between the two campsites. He displayed further contempt for the Texans by having his musicians play "Deguello," the old throat-cutting song of no quarter, to the sinister notes of which the Alamo defenders had died. Nor could he resist at least a token appearance after sending his aide to convey the twelve-pound cannon—the Gold Standard—to the island of timber separating the two military positions. Bedecked with medals and wearing his jaunty Napoleon-style headpiece, he appeared grandiloquently on a big bay foolishly exposing himself to the Texans' fire. It was an act designed to attract the attention of his feminine "guest" as well as to impress the enemy.

The Mexican cannoneers gave a good acount of themselves in the skirmish. They wounded Lieutenant

Colonel James Neill slightly and one bullet whizzed so close to General Houston, sitting on his horse near the Texas artillery, that it clipped one of his bridle reins. The Texans, returning the fire with the Twin Sisters, caught Fernando Urriza in the buttocks.

At this point Santa Anna ordered Delgado to unload the powder and ammunition for the cannon and to relinquish twenty pack mules laden with the ordnance stores to Captain Barragan. Barragan was to take the mules and retrieve the knapsacks left at the edge of New Washington. Realizing the danger of executing such an order, Delgado released only fourteen of the mules. Wisely he retained six so as to transport the ordnance supplies to camp.

After issuing his erratic order, Santa Anna again paraded his elegance in full view of the Texans before making his dramatic exit. When the Texans saw the artillery and ammunition stores unprotected, they pounded away. Their fire made a direct hit on the Mexicans' cannon, disabling it somewhat, scattered ordnance boxes, and killed two of the six mules.[34] With the remaining four animals, the Mexicans labored frenetically to transport the heavy ammunition cases from the timber island to the camp.

For approximately two hours hostilities ceased. Perhaps during the brief lull Santa Anna had Emily model the dresses his soldiers took at Harrisburg, or sample the chocolates and other delicacies that were a part of the spoils, or had the slave girl play the fine piano. Whether Emily was musically inclined or not, such a splendid instrument could not fail to impress the mulatto. Pianos were exceedingly rare in Texas at the time even though a few had been freighted in by oxcart or imported from Europe. In 1834, when the Robert Justus Klebergs immigrated from Germany and settled in Harrisburg, they had brought one.[35] The magnificent piano Santa Anna's men confiscated may very well have been the same. Mary Austin Holley, Stephen F. Austin's cousin who visited the colony in 1831, mentioned in her letters that young Lorenzo de Zavala, who fought at San Jacinto and acted as one of Santa Anna's interpreters later, played the piano and guitar to accompany his singing.[36] Not until 1855, when pianos began to replace the orchestra, did the musical instrument appear in substantial numbers in Texas.[37]

At four o'clock on April 29 hostilities were resumed. Colonel Sidney Sherman had obtained Houston's reluctant permission to command a detail of seventy volunteers to try to capture the Mexicans' cannon. Although Houston granted Sherman's request, he instructed the officer to reconnoiter with the cavalry but not to provoke a major action.[38] Sherman and his mounted men, including Secretary of War Thomas J. Rusk and privates Mirabeau B. Lamar and Walter P. Lane, were too late to take the cannon. To their disappointment, they saw it being drawn over the brow of the hill. In the cannon's place on the timber island fifty dragoons, under the command of Captain Miguel Aguirre, awaited the Texans. Sherman and his men attacked with such force that confusion ensued among the Mexicans.

Observing the action from camp, Santa Anna sent in two companies of riflemen to assist the dragoons. According to an eyewitness who observed the skirmish from the tall grass, Sherman drove the cavalry back under the guns of their main force and

> The Texians . . . were compelled to fall back and dismount to reload their rifles. The enemy perceiving their condition, at least one half on the ground, they dashed down upon them, forcing them to defend themselves as best they could, until they were again in their saddles, when they forced the enemy back a second time.[39]

In the second cavalry charge Rusk was surrounded by the enemy and would have become a fatality had Lamar not intervened. Mounted on a large stallion, Lamar charged a Mexican cavalryman to force an opening through which both men escaped.[40] As the Texans retreated, Lamar displayed additional valor. Nineteen-year-old Lane had been forced to dismount as the result of a shoulder wound. Although the wound inflicted by a Mexican lancer was slight, the young soldier was unable to defend himself against another lancer who rushed up to attack him. Noting the danger, Lamar shot the lancer.[41] Lane then jumped behind another mounted Texan and escaped. It was said that the dragoon wounded by Lamar to save the youth's life paused to salute the Texan's gallantry. Lamar reined in his horse and gracefully acknowledged the tribute.

During the exchange Sherman had sent his second in command, Major Lysander Wells, to Houston with a request for infantry support. Acting upon his own judgment, Houston declined Sherman's request,[42] and Sherman felt he had no choice but to withdraw. In the encounter two Texans were severely injured.

Later Houston accused Sherman of trying to incite a general contest in violation of his express orders. He reprimanded the dashing, younger Sherman for his heroic action, but he elevated Lamar to the rank of full colonel in recognition of his valor. Naturally General Rusk, whose life Lamar saved, endorsed the promotion. Despite Houston's disfavor, Sherman was acclaimed a hero by the men in ranks. Before leading the men in the two engagements on the twentieth, he had also captured a flatboat of supplies that Santa Anna had dispatched from New Washington on the nineteenth.[43] For the first time in three days, thanks to Sherman, the Texans enjoyed the luxuries of bread and coffee with their rations of beef.

As darkness descended on the night of April 20, the morale of the Texans reached new heights. Men in camp went from company to company soliciting volunteers to fight the next day without their wary leader's consent.[44] They were of one accord: *they would not follow further orders to retreat.* Throughout the activity Houston maintained his usual impenetrable reserve, beat tattoo on his drum, and retired. Across the grassy plain there was a veritable symphony of silence unmarred by the popping of champagne corks.

By the morning of April 21 Santa Anna was confident of victory. If possible the cockiness he demonstrated on his arrival at the site had doubled. Unlike Castrillon and Delgado, Santa Anna felt that he had made a formidable selection for the battlesite. He was convinced that he had the Texans bottled up in the low, marshy spot with all means of retreat cut off by the Buffalo Bayou and the San Jacinto River.[45] From a rise overlooking the battlefield, he trained his powerful telescope on the shabby Texans' camp and appraised it with utter disdain. The entire Texan force numbered fewer than 800 disheveled men with two small cannon. Moreover, according to Santa Anna's liaison, 150 of these had come down with measles.[46] Santa Anna's equipment was superior, his dragoons better disciplined, and the esprit de corps in camp unimpeachable.

In addition, the Mexican general's brother-in-law, Martín Perfecto de Cos, arrived at nine o'clock on the morning of April 21 with reinforcements of 300 recruits.[47] Santa Anna had hoped for 500 but the addition of 300 made an appreciable difference. Since the recruits had not slept, the Mexican commander directed them to stack their guns, remove their accoutrements, and withdraw to an adjoining grove to rest.[48] With no threat from the opposing camp, Santa Anna, who had chosen the scene of battle, would likewise choose the time. Pleased with himself, he returned to the pleasure and comfort of his rococo quarters with its sweeping view of beautiful San Jacinto Bay.

By eight o'clock that morning Houston's scouts had informed him of the approach of the Mexican reinforcements. Houston was not surprised, however. On April 18 Deaf Smith, his most capable scout, had intercepted Miguel Bachiller with General Filisola's reply to Santa Anna's request for support and had delivered it to Houston.[49] Houston had observed the troop movement and was probably aware of the rear guard's slow progress as it lagged behind. Even though Houston felt that news of the Mexican reinforcements would adversely affect his men, it made them more eager for action.

Whether Houston slept on the night preceding the battle is doubtful. More than likely he remained awake for some time in an attempt to appraise the situation and arrive at a decision. Certainly he was aware of the increasing insubordination in camp and the threat of Sherman's popularity to his leadership. He was equally aware that the men were spoiling for a fight and morale was favorable. Schooled as Houston was in the military tactics of his patron Andrew Jackson, he remained circumspect.[50] No doubt he pondered the possibility of defeat and its consequences in view of Santa Anna's reputation for butchery and his practice of giving no quarter.

Early on the morning of April 21 Houston ordered Deaf Smith to destroy Vince's Bridge, the only means of exit to the Brazos, where Santa Anna's second-in-command General Filisola was encamped.[51] The bridge over which Cos and the soldiers had traveled that morning was only eight miles from camp. Its destruction would prohibit further reinforcements from reaching the enemy and remove any means of escape for either side.

Historians disagree as to the precise time Houston decided to lead the charge on the afternoon of April 21. But before Smith and his six assistants undertook to destroy Vince's Bridge, Houston entrusted another important duty to his dependable scout. He instructed Smith to proceed to the San Jacinto River and, from an elevation between the two positions, count tent tops[52] to estimate Mexican troop strength. Smith chose courageous Walter P. Lane to assist him. While Lane held the mounts and acted as lookout, Smith trained his spyglass on the camp. The position of the rise was precariously close to the Mexican encampment, and when the enemy discovered the two scouts, the Texans had to make a run for it. They escaped and Smith reported to Houston. His estimate of Mexican troop strength at approximately 1500 men was accurate.[53]

But Smith reported more than numbers to Houston. He reported the overwhelming silence in the Mexican camp, the stacked guns, and the Mexican officers and soldiers partying with their women in their tents. Houston was aware of the presence of the *soldaderas* in the Mexican camp and knew of Santa Anna's capture of Emily. His expert espionage and reconnaissance units had kept him abreast of what had transpired at New Washington. One reference states

21

that "'After breakfast, he (Houston) climbed a tree'' . . . and "watched the slave girl serve Santa Anna breakfast. The Mexican dictator was wearing his bright red silk robe . . . . ''[54] But Houston did not know that the domestic revelry had begun so early in the day. Nor did he know the extent of it until Smith informed him.

Smith's report undoubtedly influenced Houston's decision to act and even dictated the exact strategy he would employ. At the end of Smith's detailed report, Houston said: "I hope that slave girl makes him (Santa Anna) neglect his business and keeps him in bed all day.''[55] Other events prior to the Texan attack followed in rapid succession. After Smith and his volunteers burned Vince's Bridge, Lamar was promoted and assigned to command the cavalry. Houston held his council of war from twelve noon until two o'clock; he had Lieutenant Colonel Joseph Bennett poll the men to determine whether they were ready to fight; he arranged for the music to accompany the charge; and paraded his men and aligned them in battle formation.[56]

When the Texans got into battle position not a single Mexican sentry was in view. Houston, waving his famous hat so that the flank commanders could see it, led the charge on his white stallion, Saracen. Screened by the trees and rising ground, the Texans in a formation two men deep, advanced on the run. Later the line stretched out across the prairie. As one account describes the battle:

> Four o'clock, Houston raised his sword, turned his white stallion toward the Mexican

camp. The 783 men surged forward—first in column, then in a long, thin line that swept like a scythe through the tall prairie grass.⁵⁷

The Texans held their fire until they were within point-blank range. Twenty paces from the enemy barricade Houston shouted the order: "Kneel! Shoot low! Fire!"⁵⁸ He continued to caution his men to hold their fire and to aim low. Why did he keep insisting that the men fire only at extremely close range and order them to kneel and shoot low? The answer is obvious: Houston knew that the Mexican targets were *horizontal*, not *vertical*.

Caught by total surprise in the midst of their afternoon dissipation, guns stacked and no guard on duty, the Mexicans offered only semi-resistance.⁵⁹ Pandemonium ensued. Instead of defending themselves, most of the soldiers tried to escape to the safety of Vince's Bridge. At the spot where the burned bridge had spanned the stream the bayou was wide and deep and, therefore, difficult to ford. As a result, many of the Santanistas, attempting to escape through the boggy marshes, made prime targets for the pursuing Texans. ⁶⁰ Shouting their battle cry, "Remember the Alamo! Remember Goliad!" (which Houston later attributed to Sidney Sherman),⁶¹ the Texans scattered Mexican corpses all the way from the enemy campsite across the prairie to Vince's Bayou—a distance of eight miles. Within the fewest minutes the assault had deteriorated into a veritable orgy of wanton slaughter with the Texans resorting to the use of knives, pistols, shotguns, and the butts of their rifles for clubs. It was the Texans' vendetta for the massacres of the Alamo and of Goliad. The bloodbath persisted in spite of the fact that Houston, whose horse was shot from under him twice, tried to stop it and restore discipline. Dr. N.D. Labadie, a participant in the battle, states in his account in *The Texas Almanac 1857-1873* that Houston shouted at the Texans: "Parade, men! Parade, men!" When the Texans ignored the order and continued killing Santanistas, Houston implored them, "Gentlemen! Gentlemen! Gentlemen!" until a few turned to listen. Whereupon he told them, "Gentlemen, I applaud your bravery. But damn your manners!"

Another soldier, Private Bob Hunter, who is also distinguished in Texas history for his grammatical lapses and original spelling, states that Houston ordered his men to take prisoners. Hunter's version asserts that Mexican bodies lay

> 3 and 4 deck around the 12-pounder. They did not git to fire there cannon but 3 times. Our men then took there gun loded it & turned it on them & shot them with there gun & they wanted to giv up. Gen'r'l Houston giv orders not to kill any more but to take prisners. Capt Easlin (William Mosby Eastland) said Boys take prisners, you now how to take prisners, take them with the but of yor guns, club guns, & remember the Alamo, remember Labaher, & club guns, right & left, & nock there ——— damn brains out.
>
> The Mexicans would fall down on there knees & say me no Alamo, me no Labaher . . . .

As soon as Houston tried to halt the killing, Secretary of War Rusk, realizing that his friend was seriously wounded, rode forward and replaced him in command. Quickly he countermanded Houston's order with his own: "If we stop, we are cut to pieces. Don't stop. Go ahead. Give them hell."[62] General Rusk restored discipline and later brought 250 Mexican prisoners into camp at Buffalo Bayou.[63] As the result of an ankle wound inflicted by a Mexican *escopeta* Houston was forced to retire from the battlesite.[64]

Providing the music to accompany the attack were three fifers—Frederick Lemsky, John Beebe, and Luke Bust—and a drummer, the free black man Hendrick Arnold,[65] who also served as a spy with Deaf Smith. To the spirited tempo of two nineteenth-century love songs, Texas certified her independence from Mexico. The songs were Thomas Moore's "Will You Come To The Bower?" which has long been accepted as the official music, and the old folksong "The Girl I Left Behind," which Walter P. Lane insisted was used.[66] Contemporary historians are inclined to honor the word of Lane, who went on to distinguish himself in both the Mexican and Civil wars—a patriot whose spectacular bravery earned him a promotion to the rank of brigadier general.[67] Houston probably contacted Lemsky and Arnold first and the two fifers organized the little group.

There is some divergence of opinion on the time Houston ordered the musicians to begin. But Private John S. Menifee, one participant, states that the army "Marched upon the enemy with the stillness of death.

25

No fife, no drum, no voice was heard, until at 200 yards . . ."⁶⁸ Most authorities concur that Houston had his army in formation before signalling the musicians to start playing. It is reasonable to assume that he did not give the signal until after the order to charge so as to take advantage of the surprise attack.

Why were the particular songs chosen? "Will You Come To The Bower?" was a popular tune of the time, and no doubt each of the four musicians could play it after a fashion. "The Girl I Left Behind" was also well-known. There is, moreover, the probability that the musicians contacted hurriedly for the event had a repertoire of only the two songs that the four could play. Consequently, it is likely that Houston left the decision up to the musicians themselves. Undoubtedly, Houston, with his innate sense of destiny, was thinking of the "pomp and circumstance" which would attach to the battle in later years. Confident of victory at last, Houston desired the additional drama of music to underscore the event. Assuredly he did not expect the Texans, inscrutable of face, rifles trailing, and bowie knives held in their teeth, to keep step to the music. The music at San Jacinto, regardless of all the strategic uses of such instrumentation in warfare, was that something extra for posterity—the icing on the cake of victory—the validation of an empire in eighteen minutes.

Various adaptations of the two pieces of music exist. The texts transcribed here conform closely to the versions used at San Jacinto. Moore's "Will You Come To The Bower?" is quoted from *Amateur's*

Songbook published in Boston in 1843. The version of "The Girl I Left Behind" is an authentic one collected by Ethel Chauncey O. Moore and published in *Ballads and Folk Songs of The Southwest* in 1964.

WILL YOU COME TO THE BOWER?

Will you come to the bower I have shaded for you?
I've decked it with roses all spangled with dew,
Will you, will you, will you, will you
Come to my bower?

There under the bower on sweet roses you'll rest,
While a smile lights the eyes of the girl I love best.
Will you, will you, will you, will you
Smile, my beloved?
Will you, will you, will you, will you
Smile, beloved?

But the roses so fair will not rival your cheek,
Nor the dew be so sweet as the vows we shall speak.
Will you, will you, will you, will you
Speak my beloved?
Will you, will you, will you, will you
Speak, my beloved?

We'll swear 'mid the roses we never shall part,
Thou fairest of roses, thou queen of my heart
Will you, will you, will you, will you
Won't you, my love?
Will you, will you, will you, will you
Won't you, my love?[69]

THE GIRL I LEFT BEHIND

*There was a rich old farmer
Lived in the country close by,
He had a lovely daughter;
On her I cast my eye.
She was handsome and good looking,
Both proper, straight, and fair.
There was not a girl in the country round
With her I could compare.*

*I asked her if she'd be willing
For me to cross those plains.
She said she'd be willing
If I'd come back again.
She said that she'd be true to me
Till death did prove unkind;
So we kissed, shook hands, and parted,
And I left that girl behind.*

*I left the state of Texas;
To New Mexico I was bound.
I landed in Santa Fe city;
I viewed the place all round.
Money and work were plentiful;
The boys to me were kind;
But the only thought that I ever had
Was that girl I left behind.*

*One day I was riding
Across the public square,
The mail hack was approaching;*

> *I met the driver there.*
> *He handed me a letter*
> *Which gave me to understand*
> *That the girl that I had left behind*
> *Had married another man.*
>
> *I turned my horse all round and round,*
> *Not knowing what to do;*
> *But I read a little farther,*
> *And it proved the words were true.*
> *Labor I have laid over;*
> *It's gambling I've designed.*
> *I'll ramble this wide world over*
> *For the girl I left behind.*
>
> *Come, all you reckless and rambling boys*
> *Who have listened to my song,*
> *If it's done no good, sir,*
> *I'm sure it's done no wrong.*
> *But when you court a pretty girl,*
> *Just marry her when you can;*
> *For if you ever cross those plains,*
> *She'll marry another man.*[70]

That evening, when the captured Santanistas surrounded huge fires under guard in the absence of a stockade, the Texans compiled statistics. Official Texan figures listed 630 Mexicans killed, 208 wounded, and 730 taken prisoner, making a total of 1568.[71] Various estimates of the Texan strength place the number from 800 to 900. Notwithstanding, Houston in his official report to President Burnet cited the number of men under his command as 783.[72] This figure, evidently omitting the sick or ineffective men, could have been slightly high. Rusk's estimate was 750 "effective men."[73] Only two Texans were killed: Private Lemuel Stockton Blakley and Second Lieutenant George A. Lamb.[74] Seven others died later of injuries, among them Rusk's courageous young aide, Dr. Junius William Motley. Approximately twenty Texans were wounded.[75] Santa Anna's army had been wiped out, but the Mexican commander himself was not among the prisoners or the wounded.

At the first discharge of gunpowder, Santa Anna had reverted to type. He repeated his New Washington performance except for a few disparities, the two main ones being that he was afoot this time and not in uniform. In his attempt to escape he rushed out of his tent, wringing his hands, completely disoriented.[76] He made no effort to issue an order. Seeing his plight, an aide offered him Old Whip, the magnificent stallion that had been commandeered from the Allen Vince ranch the preceding day. Santa Anna jumped on the animal and dashed away from the site at breakneck speed.[77]

Santa Anna fled wearing only red morocco slippers, a linen shirt with diamond studs, and white silk drawers.[78] Certainly his attire was hardly that expected of an emperor of a nation and the commander of the Mexican troops who considered himself the counterpart of Napoleon. In his flight he managed to take along a fine gray vest with gold buttons, which he was probably wearing, a bed sheet, a box of the Harrisburg chocolates, and a gourd water bottle half full.[79] Santa Anna's ignominious retreat only added to the demoralization of his men, who scurried aimlessly in all directions.

A few of the Mexican officers, among them General Castrillón and Colonel Delgado, tried to rally their soldiers with indifferent success.

When the smoke of battle lifted, evidence remained to corroborate that the party in Santa Anna's tent had been in full swing. George Erath, a Texan who later guarded the commander's baggage, was one of the first to confirm the fact. He discovered unmistakable evidence, part of which consisted of cooked gourmet edibles and "baskets of champagne."[80] Erath said that Santa Anna's personal effects comprised such luxuries "as a European prince might have taken with him in the field."[81] No wonder the Texan concluded that much of the victory at San Jacinto was traceable to "Santa Anna's voluptuousness." In the onslaught Castrillon was slain, Almonte taken prisoner, but Santa Anna and Cos were still missing by nightfall of April 21.

As it transpired, Santa Anna was captured almost by accident the following day. The searching detachment, headed by Colonel Edward Burleson, had rounded up two or three cowering Mexicans hiding in the vicinity of the burned bridge on the morning of April 22. While Colonel Burleson proceeded toward the head of the bayou, accompanied by most of the searching party, a patrol of six men decided to abandon the search and return to camp. These were Joel Robison, who could speak a smattering of Spanish, Sergeant James Austin Sylvester, color-bearer of his company, Privates S. R. Bostick, Alfred Miles, Charles Thompson, and Joseph Vermillion.[82]

As the men reached a point between the charred bridge and the Lynchburg ferry, where the tufted sedge grew shoulder-high, Sergeant Sylvester saw some deer and reined in his mount to take aim. Before he could fire, however, something moving in the sedge frightened the animals away. Seconds later the head of a man topped by a crude cap of hides emerged above the marsh grass. The contingent hauled the man out into the open. Besides the foul smelling cap, he was garbed in a faded blue cotton round jacket and trousers of coarse white domestic, the type of clothing slaves of the time habitually wore.[83]

Apparently Santa Anna had given Old Whip his head and the homing instinct influenced the animal to take him to the Vince ranch. With a pathological fear of water, Santa Anna had attempted to ford the bayou, in his effort to reach General Filisola on the Brazos, and had mired the horse. When he was found the Mexican general had lost his sense of direction and was traveling toward the Texan camp. Later the muddy animal he had been forced to abandon was recovered unharmed. Santa Anna recounted the incident in this manner:

> I alighted from the horse and concealed myself in a thicket of dwarf pine. Night came, and

I crossed the creek with water up to my waist. I found a house that had been abandoned (a slave's cabin on the Vince ranch) and some articles of clothing, which enabled me to change my apparel. At eleven a.m. the next day, April twenty-second, I was crossing a large place and my pursuers overtook me.[84]

When taken captive the fugitive dictator was wearing his diamond-studded shirt under the blue smock. The fate of his elegant vest is not clear unless Santa Anna had used it to barter for some favor which he did not reveal. When Sylvester first discovered the Mexican officer thus attired in a slave's discarded apparel, Santa Anna was carrying a bundle made of his sheet, his wet underwear, and his water bottle. He had draped a saddle blanket serape-fashion around his shoulders. His feet were bare and bleeding from brambles.[85] When ordered out of the tall sedge, Santa Anna ran feebly a few paces before falling to the ground covering himself with his dirty blanket. Private Bostick would have disposed of him on the spot, but Sylvester interposed. For a while the detachment forced their prisoner to stumble along painfully ahead as Private Miles prodded him from behind with a Mexican lance. But the pathetic Santa Anna kept falling down and so Joel Robison, a man of compassion who had also prevailed against the killing of the captive, let the bedraggled dictator ride behind him into camp.[86] Although the six-man patrol suspected that their prisoner was an officer because of his fine shirt, Santa Anna would not disclose his identity.

Santa Anna's identity was not definitely established until he was brought before General Houston on April 22 around two o'clock in the afternoon. When the Texans arrived with their prisoner wearing the nondescript clothes and riding behind Joel Robison, Mexican soldiers exclaimed *"El Presidente! El Presidente!"*[87] Only then did the famous captive acknowledge that he was Santa Anna and request that he be accorded the courtesies of war commensurate with his rank.

As soon as the Texans learned of Santa Anna's identity they wanted to kill him. Apprehensive of the hostility displayed and unaware of Houston's intentions to preserve his life, Santa Anna gave the Masonic distress signal. It required the combined efforts of Houston, Rusk, and John W. Wharton—the founder of the Masonic Lodge in Texas—to restrain the Texans from killing Santa Anna.[88] Before the Mexican commander could engage in the two-hour interview with Houston, in which Moses Austin Bryan, General Almonte, and young Lorenzo de Zavala took turns as interpreters, he chewed plugs of opium to regain his composure.[89]

The capture of General Cos the next day, the final release of Santa Anna and his return to Mexico, by way of Washington, D.C. (to fight the Americans again in the Mexican War), and the terms of the secret and public Treaties of Velasco ending the conflict are too well known to justify inclusion here.[90]

And what became of Emily? The slave girl survived the Battle of San Jacinto and lived to relate the details of her role in it to her master and benefactor, Colonel Morgan.[91] Since there is no record of anyone having seen Emily at the battlesite after the attack, it is logical to believe that she returned to New Washington—a distance of only seven or eight miles—soon after the assault. The woman was not a product of plantation life in the Deep South. She was an eastern import with extraordinary intelligence and sophistication.[92] It is also feasible that a Texan gave her safe escort back to Morgan's Point. Deaf Smith, the free black man Hendrick Arnold, and other Texas spies knew her as they had obtained intelligence from the indentured servants of New Washington. Also the Morgan plantation had been a source of provisions for the Texas army.

It is believed that Emily told her story to Colonel Morgan on April 23 when he and Vice President Lorenzo de Zavala—father of the young de Zavala, who fought at San Jacinto—stopped at New Washington en route from Galveston with reinforcements and supplies for Houston's army.[93] The two men had embarked on the *Cayuga* unaware that the battle had been fought on April 21. They obtained their first news of the victory from the servants on Morgan's plantation.[94]

Later Emily was issued a passport and permitted to return to her home in New York.[95] Apparently Emily's role at San Jacinto influenced Colonel Morgan to grant her her freedom. Later Morgan purchased the gaudy candy-striped marquee reminiscent of his indentured servant and presented it to Samuel Swartwout, customs collector of the port of New York.[96] Naturally Morgan passed Emily's story on to others, including his English friend, the ethnologist William Bollaert, to whom he quoted her verbatim.

Even though early Texas histories and various nineteenth-century documents substantiate Emily Morgan's presence at San Jacinto, later historians preferred either to ignore it or treat the incident as myth. One assumption for this inequity is that until comparatively recent times historians and writers of textbooks would not permit the idea of sex to tarnish any account of the celebrated battle. On the contrary, these historians attached to their printed reports of the Battle of San Jacinto something akin to sacred aura. Another explanation is that Texas history was usually offered to students of grammar school level where allusion to the "birds and bees" was avoided until the psychology of modern sex education for children came into vogue. Consequently, historians clung to the absurd *siesta* fallacy without bothering to rationalize why a man—even a Mexican general—would take a nap in a diamond-studded shirt!

It is also entirely probable that male chauvinism (the insistence that the laurels of San Jacinto belong only to such heroes as Houston, Rusk, and Lamar) and race prejudice (the notion that no such role should be attributed to a woman of color in a predominantly white society) were contributing factors to the censorship of Emily.

Thus it remained for William Bollaert, the English ethnologist, to be among the first to report the incident. A frequent visitor to Texas,, Bollaert kept diaries of his experiences from December, 1841, to April 11, 1844. However, for some obscure reason the extensive Bollaert Papers did not attract attention in America until 1902. Not until 1956 did a major portion of the material appear in a book titled *William Bollaert's Texas*, edited by W. Eugene Hollon and Ruth Lapham Butler. This work quotes an assertion made by the Englishman July 7, 1842:

> The Battle of San Jacinto was probably lost by the Mexicans owing to the influence of a mulatto girl, Emily, belonging to Colonel James Morgan. She was closeted in the tent with General Santana at the time the cry was made: 'The enemy! They come! They come!' She detained Santana so long that order could not be restored readily.[97]

Long before Bollaert's account (with which he credits James Morgan) was published, however, the story of Emily Morgan was widely circulated as an aspect of Texas folklore. Furthermore, Mexican historians have verified Emily's presence at San Jacinto for years.[98] Generally, Mexican historians categorize the slave girl as Santa Anna's "quadroon mistress during the Texas Campaign."[99] To allude to Emily Morgan as the Mexican commander's "captive slave girl" would not have reflected favorably on the "Napoleon of the West's" reputation as a national hero. Today this detail of Texas and Mexican history is especially well-known in Monterrey and Tampico, where Santa Anna is still revered.

Many persons wonder whether the lovely gold-skinned girl was not infatuated with, or at least flattered by, the attentions of the emperor of Mexico. That question must remain unanswered. However, as a member of the Morgan household and an indentured servant who came to the Mexican province from New York by choice, Emily was apparently loyal to the Morgan family and to Texas. Morgan himself had a reputation for being generous and kind and was said to have treated his indentured servants, who helped to populate his plantation, well. It is logical, then, to think that the slave girl found her home at New Washington comfortable and pleasant.

When Santa Anna captured her Emily was assisting in the loading of a flatboat with supplies for consumption by Houston's army. Though not identified by name, Emily Morgan was undoubtedly the woman of color who sent Turner, the yellow boy captured with her, to warn Houston of Santa Anna's approach. Again, despite any hypothetical attraction Emily might have felt for Santa Anna, she was a captive from the opposite side and was familiar with the *status quo*. Increasingly, the belief that Emily Morgan performed her service for her adopted home of Texas out of loyalty is gaining credence.

Regardless of motives, the results of the slave girl's performance at San Jacinto are without precedent. Not only did Emily's dalliance with Santa Anna at San Jacinto keep him occupied and cement the victory of the sixteenth decisive battle of the world, it validated an empire—the Republic of Texas—that flourished for a decade. Moreover, the victory at San Jacinto not only brought Texas into the United States but also added the future states of New Mexico, Arizona, California, Utah, Colorado, Wyoming, Kansas, and Oklahoma—a million square miles of territory that more than doubled the size of the American nation at the time.[100] Even for a most generous ladies' man, this real estate, in terms of intrinsic nineteenth-century values, had to be an all-time record as a fee for the companionship of Emily for a period of less than two days and nights. As payment by the hour for that brief time, the fee approximated a world-shattering record. The fortunes paid by the crowned heads of Europe for the favors of Madame de Pompadour and her successor, the Comtesse Du Barry, become paltry sums by comparison.

... And so they say the Yellow Rose of Texas returns to the battlesite on each recurring April 21 .... Prepared to meet her halfway is the organization of stout patriots comprised essentially of outstanding attorneys and Texas history enthusiasts, who call themselves "Sons of the Knights of the Yellow Rose of Texas (SKYRT)." Dedicated to the preservation of Emily's contribution to the victory at San Jacinto, these men have memorialized the heroine at the spot overlooking San Jacinto Bay, where she helped to win Texas' independence.[101]

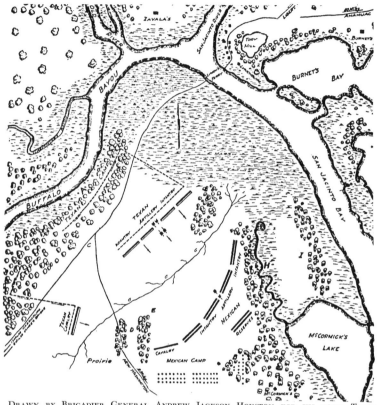

Drawn by Brigadier General Andrew Jackson Houston for his book, Texas Independence. Courtesy of The Anson Jones Press

MAP OF THE POSITIONS

OF THE TEXAN AND OF THE MEXICAN ARMIES, AT THE COMMENCEMENT OF THE BATTLE OF SAN JACINTO, AT HALF PAST THREE O'CLOCK IN THE AFTERNOON OF THURSDAY, APRIL 21, 1836.

A   HEADQUARTERS OF GENERAL HOUSTON, ON BUFFALO BAYOU
B   HEADQUARTERS OF GENERAL SANTA ANNA, IN CEDAR GROVE
C   POSITION OF TEXAN ARTILLERY, APRIL 20TH
D   POSITON OF MEXICAN ARTILLERY, ON 20TH
E   CAVALRY COMBAT, ON 20TH
F   "ISLAND OF TIMBER" USED AS SCREEN BY HOUSTON, APRIL 21ST
G   SWALE 20 FEET DEEP, CROSSED BY TEXAN LINE OF BATTLE, ON 21ST
H   DEEP AND NARROW BAYOU CROSSED BY FLEEING MEXICANS, ON 21ST
I   GROVE WHERE ALMONTE AND MANY OTHERS WERE CAPTURED ON 21ST

CHAPTER TWO

Manuscript Copy
Of The Folksong

ONE of the earliest versions of the folksong inspired by Emily Morgan is preserved in a curious manuscript copy as a part of the A. Henry Moss Papers in the Archives Division of The University of Texas at Austin. Since a special courier evidently delivered this handwritten copy to one "E. A. Jones" (no indication of a stamp or postal cancellation appears and the address is omitted), the manuscript possibly dates back to the first administration of Sam Houston as president of the Republic of Texas in 1836.

A post office department with regular mail routes did not operate in Texas until Houston's first administration, which ended in December, 1838.[1] Although the provisional government established a post office department by decree on December 12, 1835, the Congress of the Republic of Texas did not approve it until December 20, 1836.[2] During Houston's first administration John Rice Jones served as postmaster general and organized the postal system.[3] The first postal route, established in 1835, ran from San Felipe de Austin to the headquarters of

The Yellow Rose of Texas

There's a yellow rose in Texas that I am a
going to see
No other darky knows her none only me
She cryed so when I left her it like to
broke my heart And if I ever find her
we never more will part

Chorus
She is the sweetest rose of color this darky ever
knew
Her eyes are bright as diamonds they sparkee
like the dew
You may talk a bout dearest may and sing
of Rosa Lee
But the yellow rose of Texas beats the belles
of Tennessee

Where the Rio Grande is flowing and the starry skies
are bright She walks a long the river in the
quite summer night
She thinks if I remember when we parted long ago
I promised her to come back a gain and not to leave
her so
Oh now I am a going to find her for my heart
is full of woe
and we will sing the song to geather we sung so
long ago

EARLIEST KNOWN COPY OF THE SONG, ADDRESSED TO E.A. JONES.

We will play the banjo gaily and we will [sing]
The Song of yore but the
And the yellow of Pescar shall be mine for ever
more

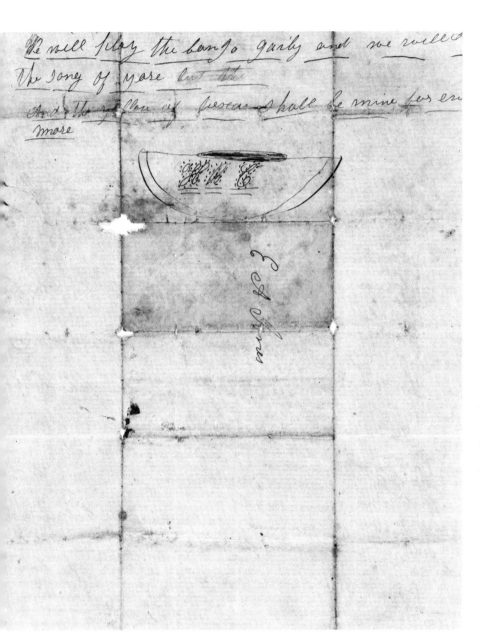

NOTE THE EMBELLISHED INITIAL & SIGNATURE AND THE FOLDING TO FORM AN ENVELOPE.
COURTESY, ARCHIVES DIVISION, THE UNIVERSITY OF TEXAS LIBRARY AT AUSTIN.

the army, to Bexar, to Velasco, and to Cantonment Jessup (in Natchitoches Parish, 379 miles from New Orleans).[4] Even so the system was funded by the government and its pedestrian-paced wagon train conveyances operated by private contractors and subcontractors left much to be desired. As a result of delays, breakdowns, and general inefficiency, many people continued to transmit mail by special courier or by travelers passing through a particular place.[5] Therefore it is logical to deduce that this early handwritten version of "The Yellow Rose of Texas" was made soon after the Battle of San Jacinto, if not shortly before.

The style of the document further identifies it with the early nineteenth century and the Republic of Texas. Markings indicate that someone folded the second sheet of the manuscript in the custom of the day to serve as the outside cover. Furthermore, the eccentricities of penmanship, frequent underscorings, and the embellished signature (H. B. C.) characterize the period of the quill pen. Especially is the extraordinary signature indicative of the date. Initials, underlined twice and decorated with dots, center a symbol suggestive of the paraph common to the era. Prominent personages of the time employed extravagant paraphs after their signatures either for emphasis or to discourage forgery. Houston's and Thomas J. Rusk's rubrics were two of the most distinctive of the period. Upon cursory examination, the symbol in this case resembles what appears to be a drawing of the pioneer Texas hat with crushed crown and reversed brim—the type of headgear Houston himself wore. Upon more thorough scrutiny, the emblem suggests a hastily sketched fourth section of a watermelon. Another possible interpretation is that it could simulate an engraved serving receptacle.

If judged by the erratic form, that is, the running of two lines together, and the inaccuracies in spelling (*darky, cryed,* and *quite* for *quiet,* etc.), the transcription represents the labors of an uneducated person. Composed from the first person point of view of a lover, the song laments the loss of his sweetheart through absence. Apparently the black man has deserted his sweetheart, and now he must find her to renew the relationship. It is interesting to note that in a comparison with the "belles of Tennessee" Emily is the superior girl. It is of further interest to note the names of other girls—"dearest May" and "Rosa Lee."

"Rose," a popular feminine name of the nineteenth century, was frequently employed in songs and poems. The flower was used to glorify young womanhood because of its obvious symbolism. In fact, the rose was the favorite symbol of the Irish poet and songwriter Thomas Moore, whose "Will You Come to The Bower?" was played at the Battle of San Jacinto.[6] It should not be surprising, then, that the phrase *The Yellow Rose of Texas* replaced the words *Emily, the Maid of Morgan's Point* in another set of original lyrics.[7]

Who was the lover? Was he real or imaginary? Could he have been one of the blacks Colonel Morgan imported from Bermuda to inhabit his little empire of New Washington in 1835? Whatever his identity, the black lover remains one of the mysteries of the legend the song has accumulated.

The complete lyrics with the lines properly divided follow:

> *There's a yellow rose in Texas*
> *That I am a going to see*
> *No other darky [sic] knows her*
> *No one only me*
> *She cryed [sic] so when I left her*
> *It like to broke my heart*
> *And if I ever find her*
> *We nevermore will part.*

Chorus:

> *She's the sweetest rose of color*
> *This darky ever knew*
> *Her eyes are bright as diamonds*
> *They sparkle like the dew*
> *You may talk about dearest May*
> *And sing of Rosa Lee*
> *But the yellow rose of Texas*
> *Beats the belles of Tennessee.*

> *Where the Rio Grande is flowing*
> *And the starry skies are bright*
> *She walks along the river*
> *In the quite [sic] summer night*

*She thinks if I remember
When we parted long ago
I promised to come back again
And not to leave her so.*

*Oh now I am agoing to find her
For my heart is full of woe
And we will sing the song togeather [sic]
We sung so long ago
We will play the banjo gaily
And will sing the song of yore
And the yellow rose of Texas
Shall be mine forevermore.*[8]

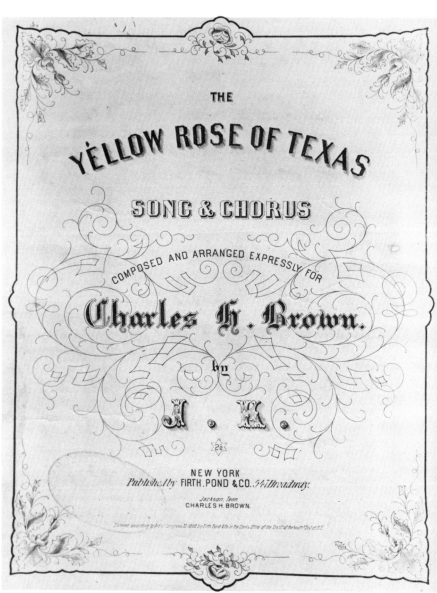

COVER OF THE FIRST VERSION, PUBLISHED IN 1858. COURTESY ARCHIVES DIVISION, TEXAS STATE LIBRARY.

CHAPTER THREE

First Copyright Edition Of The Song

THE first published edition of "The Yellow Rose of Texas" in sheet music form, including both words and score, was copyrighted September 2, 1858[1] by Firth, Pond & Company, 547 Broadway, New York, N.Y.[2] It was subsequently published in the same year by Wm. A. Pond & Company[3] and republished in 1859, 1860, 1861, and 1875.[4] By the 1860s the song had also begun to appear on broadsides and in songsters and rapidly became a favorite with blackfaced performers in America and abroad. The original Christy's Minstrels introduced the number to London audiences in the nineteenth century.[5] Simultaneously the folksong continued to be popular in various parts of the world.

The front cover of the original redaction copyrighted in 1858 states that the "Song & Chorus" was "Composed and Arranged Expressly for Charles H. Brown by J.K."[6] Brown, a vaudeville performer of Jackson, Tennessee, possibly commissioned the composition so as to incorporate it in his repertoire. It is apparent that the person enigmatically identified as

First page of the 1858 version, courtesy Archives Division, Texas State Library.

"J.K." and Brown were collaborators, even though the cover attributes the actual composition of the music to the former. Through the years the identity of the initialed composer or arranger has remained a mystery. It has been suggested that the musician so designated probably remained anonymous in conformity with the prevailing custom of the time, namely that identities of commercial arrangers employed by publishers were concealed as a matter of policy. There is no verification of this, however. Why the composer of the music of such a charming old song would desire to hide behind anonymity is puzzling. Nor is the initialed signature logical in view of the fact that the music continued to be in demand for more than two decades immediately after its publication and still retains its popularity today.

The lyrics of this early printed version are almost identical to the curious handwritten copy except for the errors in traditional form and spelling. Written in the key of B flat major to 4/4 time, the piece is both sprightly and light.

This exceedingly rare, engraved edition of "The Yellow Rose of Texas" consists of five pages, 10 by 13 inches in size. The ornate cover of the music features lacy rose designs and the back cover is blank. The valentine-like face of the sheet music, together with a specimen of the first page of the arrangement, is often reproduced in books relating to the Battle of San Jacinto and to Santa Anna personally.

Possibly no more than half a dozen copies of the original copyright edition are extant. Two of these are in the archives of the Texas State Library and the Barker Texas History Center. The remaining four are in the possession of private collectors. Former Senator Ralph W. Yarborough of Austin has one and there is another in the Texas collection of the late historian Louis Lenz of Houston. Still another released under the Firth, Pond & Company label in 1858 belongs to Clois Bennett of Austin. This first edition of "The Yellow Rose of Texas" bears the baffling annotation "Hateful rose" [sic] inscribed in pencil beneath the title of the first page. Even more enigmatic, the writing style of the two-word inscription (which spells "Rose" with a lower case letter) greatly resembles the penmanship of the manuscript copy, circa 1836-1837.

CHAPTER FOUR

A Civil War Marching Song

DURING the Civil War Confederate soldiers marched to the tune of "The Yellow Rose of Texas." Since music was an important part of the culture of the South, the men in gray sang as they went into combat. Frequently Confederate bands would strike up a familiar waltz tune or polka at the height of the battle's frenzy.

One Southern writer of the Civil War period, Maud Jeannie Fuller Young, whose son served in Hood's Texas Brigade, borrowed the melody of "The Yellow Rose of Texas" for a song she named "Song of the Texas Ranger."[1] It is quite possible, then, that some Texans, who may have been unfamiliar with the words of "The Yellow Rose of Texas" had heard the music.

One version of the song, sung by men commanded by General John B. Hood, has been recorded in the chapter "Ballads of the Civil War" in *The Dell Book of Great American Folk Songs*. Although the text has an annotation stating that the song is presented in its original form, the words are somewhat altered. For example, while the song retains the phrase "She's the sweetest rose of color," this variant substitutes the word *soldier* for *darky*.

A notable feature is a fourth stanza in which one line of the original chorus is repeated. The stanza, which is not compatible with the rest of the ballad, apparently was composed by some of General Hood's men after their defeat in Tennessee.[2]

The defeat amounted to a bloodbath. Surrounded by Union troops, General Hood and his men retreated in complete disorder. Some of the soldiers became so confused by the carnage that they felt the war was over and returned home, as the lyric indicates.

And now I'm going southward, for my heart is full of woe.
I'm going back to Georgia, to find my uncle Joe.
You may talk about your dearest May, and sing of Rosalie,
But the gallant Hood of Texas played hell in Tennessee.

The Dell songbook copyrighted in 1963 is a facsimile of a first edition released in 1881. Jim Morse edited the songbook, which contains a Foreword by the late Carl Sandburg, a well-known collector of American folk music and a guitar-playing troubadour of national stature, who once considered collaboration with J. Frank Dobie.[3] In his Foreword to the Dell songbook Sandburg declares that "the present generation in the U.S.A. has seen a tremendous upsurge of ballad and folksong research . . . . It means in part that folk ways of having fun and recreation have struck deep old-time roots."

CHAPTER FIVE
Octavo Edition Of 1906

ANOTHER original copy of the folksong in the Archives Collection of The University of Texas Library is a published octavo score copyrighted in 1906. In the key of D major with the time signature changed to ⅔, this variant is paraphrased with trills and mordents that add distinction and indicate increased respect.

Likewise released by Wm. A. Pond & Company, this arrangement, composed for a male quartet, encompasses both English and German lyrics. A musician by the name of William Dressler is credited with both the musical score and the German translation. Interestingly, in the upper left hand corner directly opposite the credit line for Dressler are the initials "J.K." Whatever the identity of this original composer, his full name still remained unknown. Of interest at this point is the fact that a previous musician's symbol of signature was at least recognized.

One of the Southwest's foremost composers, David W. Guion of Dallas, who is noted for his use of Negro folk music as thematic material, is convinced

Secular OCTAVO MUSIC.

Title	Voices	Composer/Arranger	Price
A SOUTHERN LULLABY.	Mixed Quartette	M. Seymour.	10
DOWN ON THE SANDS.	Male Voices	R. B. Shepherd.	15
OLD BLACK JOE.	Mixed Voices	C. F. Shattuck.	15
SWEET GENEVIEVE.	,, ,,	C. F. Shattuck.	15
SWEET and LOW.	Male Voices. (J. Barnby.)	W. C. Williams.	10
COME WHERE MY LOVE LIES DREAMING. (Foster)	Male	A. Claassen.	15
WAITING.	Male Voices. (Millard)	C. F. Shattuck.	25
WAITING.	Mixed Voices. (Millard)	C. F. Shattuck.	25
QUADRILLES OR COUNTRY DANCES.	Mixed Voices	J. Farmer.	25
SHE SPEAKS TO ME.		D. Prothero.	15
GOOD NIGHT BELOVED.		C. Pinsuti.	15
COME WHERE MY LOVE LIES DREAMING. (Mixed)	Female	Wm. Dressler.	20
FAR, FAR FROM OLDEN TIME.	Mixed. Male	J. Mendelsohn	10
THE DEATH IT IS THE BREEZY NIGHT.	Mixed. Male	,, ,,	10
SWEET GENEVIEVE	Male Female	Wm. Dressler	15
COAL TAR LEMON PIE.		Victor Vane.	10
OLD FOLKS AT HOME. *English & German Words.* Mixed, Male & Female Voices		arr. by Wm. Dressler.	15
DIXIE'S LAND. *English & German Words.* Mixed, Male & Female Voices		arr. by Wm. Dressler.	15
EILLEEN ALLANNA.	Male. Mixed, Female	arr. by Wm. Dressler.	10
HEBE. (Thou art my own love)	Male. Mixed. Female.	arr. by Wm. Dressler.	15
THE YELLOW ROSE OF TEXAS.	Male Voices	arr. by Wm. Dressler.	12
NELLY WAS A LADY.	Mixed Voices	arr. by Wm. Dressler.	12

NEW YORK
WM. A. POND & CO., 148 FIFTH AVENUE.
CHICAGO, ILL.   NEW ORLEANS, LA.
CHICAGO MUSIC CO., 152-154 WABASH AVE.,   L. GRUNEWALD CO., LT'D., 127 CANAL ST.

Octavo Edition published in 1906. The words are in German and English.

that the original composer of "The Yellow Rose of Texas" was a talented black man.

This octavo edition of the old song in two languages is almost identical to the early manuscript copy and the printed version of 1858, except that the handwritten copy has corrections in spelling and contains a few contractions for the sake of rhythmical smoothness.

The refrain of this intriguing rendition is identical to the other two transcriptions except for the insertion of the word *your* before "Dearest May" and the alteration of *promised* into a contraction—*promis'd*.

Only a few minor transitions mark the final stanza. Besides the corrected spelling, two or three contractions appear. Also the line *We sung so long ago* is preceded by the pronoun *That*. It is of interest to note that the folksy past participle *sung* has not been replaced by the correct, but stiff, past tense *sang*.

Since the octavo version was printed in 1906 and the German lyrics were added, it reveals that little change in the original song had occurred since its possible inception in 1836 or 1837—a span of some seventy years. Simultaneously publication of the song in German indicates that the folksong was steadily gaining a wider audience. A detail worthy of notice in the transcription is that "Dearest May" becomes "Nellie Bly," a literary girl revered in a different folksong; whereas the name "Rosa Lea," which is common to the other versions, is preserved.

IDENTITY OF "HATEFUL ROSE" UNKNOWN. NOTE LOWER CASE r IN THE CURIOUS ANNOTATION. COURTESY OF CLOIS W. BENNETT OF AUSTIN.

CHAPTER SIX

Typescript Variant Of 1930

STILL a third variant of the folksong that merits scrutiny is in the archival accessions of The University of Texas Library at Austin. This is a typescript bearing the acquisition date of May, 1930, with a notation made by Mattie Austin Hatcher, the university archivist at the time. The notation reads: "Words furnished by Mr. Wright, custodian of the Daughters of the Confederacy Museum, May 1930 . . . M.A.H."

It is reasonable to think that the original might have been filed in the Daughters of the Confederacy Museum, but a recent check reveals that no such copy exists there. This version could have been simply a personal copy which Mr. Wright shared with Miss Hatcher.

The principal innovation of this version concerns its use of Negro dialect prevalent in Texas and the South before the Civil War. Even the caption in this copy has been altered to read "The *Yaller* Rose of Texas." This datum lends support to musician David Guion's assumption that the original composer or first person to record the old folksong was a black man. For that matter, as slavery proliferated in the South, the music of the Negro supplanted an earlier reliance on English songs and melodies. Since the spontaneous music of black people became an integral aspect of Southern folklore, it could be argued that the assumption is credible.

Although some dialect pervades the lyrics, its use is not consistent. For instance, in the first stanza only three dialectical terms appear: the word *darkie* in two lines, the word *yaller* in the first line, and the contraction *I'se* in the penultimate line. In the second line of the chorus two words of dialect appear: "This *darkie eber* knew." Then, peculiarly, the correct spelling of *yellow* follows in the line next to the last instead of the jargon *yaller*. In the second—and last stanza—the first line repeats the contraction *I'se*: "But now *I'se* going to find her." The second line employs the verb *am*: "For my heart *am* full of woe." Then incongruously in the third line, there appears the correct qualifying adjective *those*, rather than the corresponding dialectical word *dem*. Additional incongruity accrues in that no other jargon except the word *yaller* appears in the next to the last line. Still even more inconsistent, the final line has no dialect and begins with the formal word *shall*.

CHAPTER SEVEN

Transcriptions By David W. Guion

TWO additional variants of the song belong to the 1930s. These transcriptions, which typify a hallmark in the song's extended history, were composed by David W. Guion and published by G. Schirmer Inc., of New York City. Guion, a prolific composer with some two hundred musical works to his credit, is famous for his variations on folksongs. In addition to his paraphrase of "The Yellow Rose of Texas," his popular concert scores comprise such old American favorites as "Turkey in the Straw," "Arkansas Traveler," "Alley Tunes," a Mother Goose suite, and innumerable others. His "Texas," a suite for both orchestra and voices, endeared Guion to lovers of Texana and won him a wide musical audience.

Almost from his boyhood days in Ballinger, Texas, where he was born in 1892, Guion has been acclaimed "as the most original . . . of those native composers who reveal America."[1] The musician-composer based his adaptation of "The Yellow Rose of Texas" on the traditional song as he remembered his parents singing it during his boyhood. According to his own statement, he had never seen a printed version of the folksong until he composed his first transcription in 1930.[2] Guion worked completely from memory and followed the first two pages of the original version quite closely in order to preserve the melody. From this point the composer inserted his own distinctive melodic effects without sacrificing authenticity. As Guion explains his procedure, he wished to compose a ballad "suitable for concert artists—and to get away from monotony." The classic composition into which he converted "The Yellow Rose of Texas" became highly successful on the concert stage in the East and was broadcast coast to coast.

Guion's second transcription was a special edition of the first. The musician's publishers released it in 1936 to commemorate the Texas centennial. Across the front cover of the music, above the title, appeared this interesting dedication:

Written in honor of the

One Hundredth Birthday of Texas

and dedicated to

President Franklin Delano Roosevelt

Aware of Guion's reputation for preserving folk music and profoundly affected by the tribute, President Roosevelt acknowledged it in a telephone call from the capital. Guion, who was then living in New York's Greenwich Village, relates with considerable

Written in honor of the One Hundredth Birthday of Texas
and dedicated to
President Franklin Delano Roosevelt

The Yellow Rose of Texas

Song
for Voice and Piano
by
David W. Guion

 High   Low

Song Orchestration Obtainable

G. Schirmer, Inc.
New York

COVER OF THE 1936 EDITION BY DAVID GUION. COURTESY DAVID W. GUION AND G. SCHIRMER, INC., NEW YORK.

Written in honor of the One Hundredth Birthday of Texas and dedicated to
President Franklin Delano Roosevelt

The Yellow Rose of Texas

Words and Music rewritten
David W. Guion

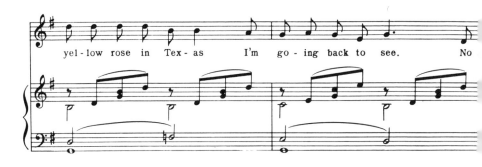

Copyright, 1936, by G. Schirmer, Inc.
International Copyright Secured
Printed in the U.S.A.

All rights reserved, including the right of public performance for profit.

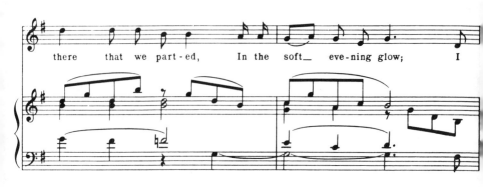

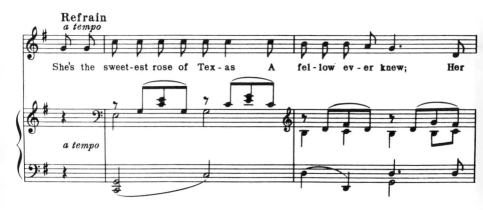

Compositions of
DAVID W. GUION

Songs

All Day on the Prairie (Texas Cowboy Song). M,E♭-F
At the Cry of the First Bird. M, D-G
The Bold Vaquero (Texas Cowboy Song). MH, C-F
Compensation. M, C♯-F♯
The Cowboy's Dream. H, E-G; ML, C-E♭
Cowboy's Meditation (Texas Range Song). ML, D-E
Creole Juanita. H, D♯-G(G♯); M, C♯-F(F♯); L, A♯-D(D♯)
De Massus an' de Missus. M, B-E
De Ol' Ark's A-Moverin'. H, D-F; L, B♭-D♭
Greatest Miracle of All. H, D-G; L, A-D
A Heart-Break. MH, F-F
Home on the Range (Texas Cowboy Song). H, D♭-F(G♭); M, C-E(F); M, B♭-D(E♭); L, G-B(C)
In Galam. M, D-E
A Kiss. M, B♭-E♭
Life and Love. M, D-F
Little Joe, the Wrangler (Texas Cowboy Song). H, E-E; L, C♯-C♯
Little Pickaninny Kid. H, B♭(C)-F; L, G-D
Lonesome Song of the Plains. H, E♭-A♭; M, C-F
Love is Lord of All. M, C-G♭
Mam'selle Marie. M, D-E

Mary Alone. L, A-D
McCaffie's Confession (Texas Frontier Bal'd). ML, C-C
Mistah Jay-bird. M, B♭-F
Mother. MH, F-F; L, D-D
My Own Laddie. M, A♭-E♭(F)
Ol' Paint. H, D-F♯; ML, B♭-D
Please Shake Dem 'Simmons Down. M, C-F
Praise God I'm Satisfied. H, E♭-E♭; L, B-B
Prayer. MH, C-F(G); L, A-D(E)
Resurrection. M, D♭-E
Return. M, D♭-B
Ride, Cowboy, Ride! H, E-G(A); M, C♯-F♯; L, B-F♯(G)
Roy Bean (Texas Frontier Ballad). ML, D-B
Run, Mary, Run. M, E♭-E♭; L, C-E
Sail Away for the Rio Grande. MH, D-F; L, B-D
Shout Yo' Glory. L, A-C
To the Sun. M, E-E
Voodoo. L, A-D
Waltzing with You in my Arms. MH, C-F(G)
Weary. M, D-G
What Shall We Do with a Drunken Sailor. H, E♭-F; ML, C-D
Wrong Livin'. L, G♯-D♯

Choruses
(4-pt. unless otherwise stated)

All Day on the Prairie. Arranged by Wallingford Riegger. Oct. 7571 (*Men's*)
All Day on the Prairie. Arranged by Wallingford Riegger. Oct. 7719 (*Men's 3-pt.*)
De Ol' Ark's A-Moverin'. Arranged by Carl Deis. Oct. 7110 (*Men's*)
Greatest Miracle of All. Arranged by Carl Deis. Oct. 7149 (*Men's*)
Home on the Range. Arranged by Wallingford Riegger. Oct. 7615 (*Men's*)
Home on the Range. Arranged by Wallingford Riegger. Oct. 7718 (*Men's 3-pt.*)
Home on the Range. Arranged by Wallingford Riegger. Oct. 7623 (*Mixed*)
Little Pickaninny Kid. Arranged by Carl Deis. Oct. 7148 (*Men's*)
Little Pickaninny Kid. (Deis-Baldwin). Oct. 9087 (*Men's*)

Piano

Alley Tunes. Three scenes from the South:
1. Brudder Sinkiller and his Flock of Sheep
2. The Lonesome Whistler
3. The Harmonica-Player

Arkansas Traveler (Old Fiddler's Breakdown). Concert transcription.
Barcarolle.
The Harmonica Player.
Minuet
Pickaninny Dance.
Prairie Dusk.
The Scissor's-Grinder.
Sheep and Goat. ("Walkin' to Pasture")
Southern Nights. (Valse)
Turkey in the Straw.
Valse Arabesque.

Orchestra

Alley Tunes. (Adolf Schmid) *Galaxy* 372
Arkansas Traveler. (Adolf Schmid) *Galaxy* 376
Arkansas Traveler. Arranged for full band by Tom Clark. *Special Edition* 67
Home on the Range, Key of E♭. *Song Orchestration* 138
Sheep and Goat ("Walkin' to Pasture"). (Adolf Schmid) *Galaxy* 321
Southern Nights (Valse-Suite). (Adolf Schmid) *Galaxy* 210
Turkey in the Straw. (Maurice Baron) *Galaxy* 221
Turkey in the Straw. Arranged for full band by John Philip Sousa. *Special Edition* 64

G. SCHIRMER, Inc. **NEW YORK**

gusto how difficult it was for the president of the United States to contact him. Since the composer worked at night, he usually slept late and left instructions not to be disturbed before nine o'clock in the morning. When the switchboard operator at his hotel (who was known at times to play practical jokes) first tried to reach Guion with the remark—"The president of the United States is on the phone"—he reprimanded the lady for waking him early and angrily clicked the telephone receiver into place.

Returning to his pillow, Guion tried to go back to sleep. But the operator called again, this time more persistently, and once more Guion hung up the telephone. When the telephone rang for the third time the composer recognized President Roosevelt's voice. "Are you the 'Home on the Range' Guion?" President Roosevelt asked in that voice made familiar to the nation through his fireside chats on radio. When assured that he had the right Guion, the president expressed his personal appreciation for the tribute. He also told Guion he had been a fan of his for years and was familiar with a number of his compositions. He named several that were favorites. Sometime later President Roosevelt invited Guion to come to Washington, D.C. and play "The Yellow Rose of Texas" for him personally at the White House.[3] The musician recalls the experience pleasantly as a highlight of his long career.

Both manuscript and original printed copies of the Texas folksong now form treasured items among the extensive Guion Collection of musical works and memorabilia in the Archives Division of the Library of The University of Texas at Austin. In recent years the musician-composer has made a gift of his immense Americana collection and original musical recordings and first editions to Baylor University.

CHAPTER EIGHT

"The Yellow Rose Of Texas" In World War II

BY the 1940s "The Yellow Rose of Texas" had passed into the category of a popular standard. Along with other folk melodies and patriotic selections, the song reappeared in community songbooks throughout the nation.[1] Notably in this later period of the song's transition many of the original folk phrases were retained but marked divergence began to appear. In a bid for wider acceptance "The Yellow Rose of Texas" had moved away from its ethnic origin, as a Negro folksong, to become part of the great American tradition.

A typical example of a World War II rendition was the Hugo Frey arrangement copyrighted in 1941 by the Robbins Music Corporation. In the version that appeared in *Victory Song Book For Soldiers, Sailors, and Marines,*[2] the traditional, straight line verson in G major and $\frac{4}{4}$ time retains much of the original phraseology. The first line of the Frey variant and that of the crude handwritten copy from the A. Henry Moss Papers in the library at The University of Texas at Austin are identical. The second line changes slightly to

> *I'm going there to see.*

Although the heroine of the song remains "the sweetest rose of color," the hero has become a *fellow*, displacing the folk term *darky*. The fourth line departs from the original "No one only me" to read

> *Nobody only me.*

The fifth line duplicates that of the early version with the exception that *cried* is spelled correctly:

> *She cried so when I left her.*

In the next line the pronoun *my* loses out to *her*, making the phrase

> *It like to broke her heart.*

Instead of "And if I ever find Her" in the original, the eighth line alters to read

> *And if we ever meet again.*

The final line of the first verse matches that of the handwritten song except that *shall* replaces the less formal auxiliary verb *will* before *part*:

> *We nevermore shall part.*

The refrain of the 1941 transcription adheres to the old handwritten copy with even fewer changes. However, "This darky ever knew" changes to

A fellow ever knew.

The two succeeding lines, in which appear the familiar similes involving *diamonds* and *dew,* remain precisely the same. But "You may talk about dearest May" is edited to read

You may talk about your dearest maids.

Except for a change in the spelling of "Rosa Lee" the rest of the chorus follows the original word for word.

The second stanza repeats the first two lines of the earlier version, then replaces the singular pronoun *she* with the plural *we* before the verb *walked.* The following line corrects the spelling of *quiet.* The succeeding phrase becomes more meaningful with the introducing of the girl's quotations. The adverb *when*, opening the next line of the old version, is truncated; and the two concluding lines of the lyric end the quoted reminiscence from the girl's point of view in place of the lover's as in the original. Thus the quatrain runs

She said if you Remember,
We parted long ago,
You promised to come back again
And never leave me so.

Even fewer emendations mark the third stanza of Frey's transcription. In fact, one of them may well be a questionable change. The lover goes *back* to reunite with his sweetheart, he himself will *pick* the banjo, not *play* it as does the man in the handwritten copy; the couple will vocalize *songs,* not just *the song*; and the relationship will exist *forevermore.* The most notable editing here focuses on the replacing of *Shall* in the last line with the awkward contraction *She'll*, giving the stanza an unnecessary error in syntax.

Obviously there were other variants of the song during the World War II period as the folksong increased in popularity and continued in the oral tradition. Also during World War II "The Yellow Rose of Texas" began to exceed national boundaries and take on international import as soldiers, sailors, airmen, and marines sang it at their combat posts and battle stations in various parts of the world. The song's catchy tempo and ease of rendition helped servicemen to escape from battle fatigue and combat jitters. One naval officer, whose base was on Saipan in the South Pacific, related this extraordinary experience:

> During World War II, when I was in the U.S. Navy in the South Pacific, I had under my command on the Island of Saipan about a hundred black sailors, most of whom were from Texas. Twenty or twenty-five of these fellows organized a glee club, and they were *good*. One of the songs they delighted in singing was THE YELLOW ROSE OF TEXAS—maybe because they were from Texas and I was a Texan. Their voices were wonderful and beautiful. We operated an airstrip, but we had also a lot of

about 200 prisoners (Japanese marines and regular soldiers) whom we worked on the roads and runways. Among these prisoners were a dozen who could speak English, one of whom was a graduate of UCLA, and some of my black boys served as guards and work supervisors of the prisoners. Before I knew it, some of these English-speaking prisoners were singing in the glee club, and when I found out about it, I did nothing to interfere. It was a most unusual sight though to see and hear all these fellows singing THE YELLOW ROSE OF TEXAS... Somewhere—packed away—I have pictures of the whole group and I've got to get them out some day and re-live those hard and difficult and unusual times.[3]

National Emblem of Mexico.

CHAPTER NINE

Reprint Of The First Edition

IT is significant that by the end of World War II, the old folksong reemerged in the form in which it was first copyrighted in 1858. Such a revival typifying a return to traditional values, lost or misplaced during the war, was the transcription of "The Yellow Rose of Texas" in *Round-Up Memories* subtitled "Songs of The Hills and Range."

Shapiro, Bernstein & Co., of Radio City Music Hall, New York, published the series of fifteen songs in 1946. The series was compiled and edited by Bud Skidmore for voice and piano and included guitar diagrams and chords. The music for "The Yellow Rose of Texas" is attributed to Robert C. Haring. Above Haring's byline appears, interestingly enough, the notation "By J. K.", thus giving at least a nod of recognition to the initialed composer of the first published edition. Across the top of the first sheet of music appears this explanation: "This is the original song as published in 1858, and that has survived throughout the years. In recent times the words have occasionally been sung to a different melody. There is no clue to the writer other than the initials J. K." Although the annotation speaks for itself, the assertion that *the words have occasionally been sung to a different melody* is a fascinating understatement. The annotation could have stated that different words have been adapted to the original melody.

"The Yellow Rose of Texas" appears with old-time favorites emblematic of early Americana and typical of nineteenth-century nostalgia. Among the songs are "Home on The Range," "The Last Round-Up," "Empty Saddles," and "Wagon Wheels." Since song titles are listed on the face of the volume alphabetically, a number bearing the extraordinary caption of "The Cross-Eyed Cowboy On The Cross-Eyed Horse" heads the list and "The Yellow Rose of Texas" is wedged between "When It's Lamp Lightin' Time In The Valley" and "You're The Only Star In My Blue Heaven."

But the important point is that a meticulous phrase-by-phrase comparison does indeed reveal that the lyrics of "The Yellow Rose of Texas" in *Round-Up Memories* are identical to those of the first published edition of 1858 attributed to the enigmatic "J. K."

CHAPTER TEN

The Mitch Miller Adaptation

UNTIL 1955 David W. Guion's concert transcription of "The Yellow Rose of Texas" was the best known version. However, in that year Mitch Miller recorded an arrangement of the folksong by Don George for Columbia Records and further popularized it on his sing-along television show. Miller, a well-known television personality, had played first chair oboe for the CBS Symphony for twelve years and had served as artist and repertoire director of the pop music division of Columbia Records since 1950. Undoubtedly the Don George-Mitch Miller version eclipsed Guion's concert transcription in popularity.

More sophisticated than its antecedents and also tailored to the taste of the contemporary dancing audience, the reproduction of the song by Mitch Miller has won wide acceptance. The Don George-Miller version sacrifices much of the old song's original charm in its elimination of some of the folk aspects characteristic of the variants bearing the initials of the mysterious "J. K." Despite this fact, some of the traditional phrases defy improvisation and are repeated

The Mitch Miller Adaptation, published in 1955.

COPYRIGHT PLANETARY MUSIC PUBLISHING CORP., 1955, ALL RIGHTS RESERVED, USED BY PERMISSION.

in this extremely modern reproduction. For instance, the simple, fresh beginning is the same:

> *There's a yellow rose in Texas*
> *That I am going to see.*

The folk idiom remains unchanged in the lines:

> *She cried so when I left her*
> *It like to broke my heart*
> *And if I ever find her,*
> *We nevermore will part.*

The second and fourth lines, however, depart from the original to read

> *Nobody else could miss her,*
> *Not half as much as me*

making the ungrammatical *me* rhyme with *see*.

The chorus, wherever possible, is modernized, with the first line "She's the sweetest rose of color" becoming

> *She's the sweetest little rosebud*

and "This darky ever knew" altered to read

> *That Texas ever knew.*

But the lines containing the apt similes:

> *Her eyes are bright as diamonds.*
> *They sparkle like the dew*

remain unchanged. As a matter of fact, these two lines remain unchanged in all texts of the song. In Miller's version "Clementine" replaces "dearest May," while the name "Ros-a-lee" is retained with updated spelling. Also the final alliterative line of the original "Beats the belles of Tennessee" becomes the more personal emotional line

> *Is the only girl for me.*

The only alteration of the almost perfect lyric involving the Rio Grande is that "She thinks if I remember" becomes

> *I know that she remembers,*

shifting the point of view from the third person to the first and replacing the present tense *thinks* with the verb *know*. The succeeding line "When we parted long ago" undergoes no change, while the line "I promised to come back again" now reads

> *I promised to return.*

The original wording "And not to leave her so" is preserved. Moreover, once again in the concluding stanza the prediction of a happy ending finds the "Yellow Rose of Texas" likely to be reunited with her lover. Miller retains some phrases of the original, as certain parts did not improve with improvisation.

Even so, the music published for Miller by the Planetary Music Publishing Corporation of New York and identified by the photograph of the band leader on the cover in a Confederate uniform signals a marked departure from other versions. Don George, the arranger, and Miller returned to the key of B flat major, used in the early printed version of 1858. However, their music features a contemporary technique that converts the charming old folksong into a popular standard.

CHAPTER ELEVEN

Boogie Woogie Transcription Of 1956

IN 1956 a simple boogie woogie transcription of "The Yellow Rose of Texas," suitable for elementary piano students, appeared. The music was arranged by John W. Schaum and published by Belwin, Inc., of Rockville Centre, Long Island, New York. This version composed for young performers further testifies to the song's continued appeal to people of all ages.

The cover of the sheet music of the 1956 version shows a yellow Texas longhorn and a yellow rose sketched in the lower left-hand corner. The face of the piece carries two notations: "traditional" and "piano solo."

The two-page arrangement, written in the key of C in 4/4 tempo, consists of only one verse followed by a chorus. While the original first line is retained:

There's a yellow rose in Texas,

the next six lines are identical to the Frey version. However, instead of Frey's "And if we ever meet again," the seventh line restores the earlier phraseology of the original

> *And if I ever find her,*

which is followed by

> *We nevermore will part,*

with the informal *will* replacing the formal *shall.*

In the chorus the old familiar beginning line "She's the sweetest rose of color" is altered to become

> *She's the sweetest rose in Texas.*

Thus the rose becomes both a lower case word and a metaphor instead of a girl's name. To replace Frey's "A fellow ever knew," the next line is edited to read

> *I ever, ever knew—*

and is less than an improvement.

The two succeeding lines, in which the *diamonds* and *day* similes are employed, remain identical to Frey's version. The fifth line of the chorus departs surprisingly from other variants to introduce the name of a new girl, "Clarabel:"

> *You may talk about your Clarabel.*

And the next line changes the spelling "Rosa Lea" to one word "Rosalee." The line "But the Yellow Rose of Texas" remains and is followed by the emended wording

> *She is the girl for me.*

This version represents a complete departure from the original "Beats the belles of Tennessee." Thus the boogie woogie version of "The Yellow Rose of Texas" is more than a delightfully refreshing easy-to-play piano piece. It reflects a complete departure from the original Negro folksong.

Postscript

Undoubtedly dusty archival files and musty attics will yield additional versions of the song "The Yellow Rose of Texas." However, the many redactions already in existence testify to the folksong's universal appeal. The persistent reappearance of the old Texas tune in original dress is reassuring. Moreover, despite the different adaptations into which the popular song has emerged, it is safe to predict that serious interpreters of folk music will favor the original in the oral tradition as it was inspired by the beautiful girl Emily Morgan—heroine of the Texas Revolution, whose saga focuses on San Jacinto and whose spirit lives from generation to generation in the hearts of patriotic Texans.

The Santa Anna Legend

General Santa Anna, circa 1837.

The Santa Anna Legend

A LEGEND involving the background of the Mexican General Antonio López de Santa Anna defeated by Texans at the Battle of San Jacinto, April 21, 1836, is still collecting moss. The legend surfaced briefly after the famous battle only to be quickly suppressed. Hung on a slender framework of historic fact, the tradition is provocative. Mrs. Martha (Sanders) Reiner, a schoolteacher of Fairfield, Ohio, had the story as it was passed down from her paternal grandmother. The late Irvin S. Cobb, American humorist and actor, whose account evolved from his maternal grandfather, corroborates the legend in his autobiography *Exit Laughing* published in 1941. Except for minor discrepancies, the essential difference in the two versions is the spelling of the name of Sanders. Cobb adds a *u*, making the name Saunders. Subsequent redactions of the legend have been published in the Louisville *Courier Journal* and other periodicals.

One Nathaniel Saunders, from whose ancestral line both Mrs. Reiner and Cobb stem, migrated from Spotsylvania County, Virginia, to Kentucky at the close of the American Revolution. Saunders and his young wife, Sarah Pattie, settled at Forks of Elkhorn, near Frankfort. Nathaniel, who had served in the Revolution as an Indian scout and spy, maintained a close association with the tribesmen of the territory. Kentucky did not become a state until 1792. This family history is verified by the early historian Richard H. Collins in his *History of Kentucky* published in 1874.

The Saunders had eight children, their oldest being born in 1779 and their youngest in 1798. Presumably, in addition to these, an illegitimate son was born —the offspring of Saunders and an Indian mistress. At this point history ends and legend begins.

Born at some time between 1779 and 1798, the son—half-Indian and half-white—was taken into the Saunders home and christened Nathaniel for his father. From childhood Mrs. Reiner remembers that precursors in their investigations of early Mexican history discovered the family relationship in the American paternity of Santa Anna and references to his boyhood spent in the environs of Frankfort. It was said that some of the Sa[u]nders descendants of earlier years bore a remarkable resemblance to photographs of the Mexican general.

According to the legend, from his childhood the boy Nathaniel acquired the nickname of Bull because of his violent temper and unusual physical strength. As he reached adolescence, Bull became incorrigible and posed a problem to both the family and the community.

Finally, to resolve their difficulty, the Saunders managed to get Bull admitted to West Point, possibly in the institution's infancy or at some time before the school was reorganized in 1812. At its inception the United States Military Academy had several false starts. It was established, abandoned, reestablished, then sadly languished. When West Point was first founded in 1802, it opened as an apprentice school for engineers with only ten students. After it was restructured it adopted a four-year curriculum designed to train cadets for military careers. It was said that admission requirements during the school's first decade of operation were extremely lax. Students were admitted without appointment or taking entrance examinations. At the time of Bull Saunders' ostensible enrollment "cadets" were said to range in age from twelve to thirty-four.

At the academy Bull Saunders excelled in military strategy but failed in the exercise of discipline. Hostile and uncooperative, he was unpopular. Then in the second year he got into serious trouble. Before the year ended, the daughter of the operator of a ferryboat between Garrison and the Point confided to her father that Cadet Saunders had violated her. Threats ensued, and only a short time later the ferryman's body was found floating in the Hudson River. Blows to the head had accounted for the death.

Though Bull denied to a fellow student that he had committed the crime, he was a prime suspect. However, before he could be arrested and brought to trial, Cadet Saunders disappeared mysteriously from the campus. Under the existing circumstances, compounded by racial prejudice and his unfavorable reputation, Cadet Saunders felt that his chances for a fair trial were poor. Moreover, his father's race had rejected him and he had no friends. It was said that at this time he developed a bitter animosity against all Americans and vowed to seek revenge.

Consequently, the half-breed youth hastily collected a few belongings and climbed the Storm King mountains behind West Point. Soon he found himself (in the language of the Cobb account) penetrating "the wild country of the Southwest." Fortunately for the fugitive, most of the area was still Indian country at the time. Swarthy of complexion and black haired, Bull could easily pass for a young brave of one of the many Indian tribes inhabiting Kentucky. Nor was his familiarity with several Indian dialects wasted in the venture.

When Bull arrived in Mexico, if indeed he did later masquerade as Santa Anna, is uncertain. In his autobiography, *The Eagle*, edited by Ann Fears Crawford and published in 1967, Santa Anna states that his career dated from 1810, when he joined the royalist army of New Spain at the age of fourteen. This would tend to fix the time of his arrival in Mexico by that date, or before, and the year of his birth at 1796. In view of the many inaccuracies in Santa Anna's account, recognized by historians generally and believed by editor Crawford to have been intentional, little credence can be placed in these data. It is more probable that Santa Anna was sixteen in 1810. In the same chapter in *The Eagle* the Mexican general neglects to divulge either his place of birth or his parents' names. He disposes of his parentage by stating simply that he joined the army with his "'parents' blessing."

Historians concur that Santa Anna spent five years, from 1810 to 1815, policing Indian tribes in the *Provincias Internas*—the Interior Provinces. At this time the Interior Provinces of New Spain were divided into two military districts—Western and Eastern—both subject to viceregal authority. The Eastern Interior Provinces, with which Santa Anna was involved, consisted of Texas, Nuevo Leon, Coahuila, and Nuevo Santander, later called Tamaulipas. Santa Anna's employment in the Eastern Interior Provinces would indicate that he had had earlier military training before reaching Mexico, or prior to the year 1810, to qualify for the exacting and hazardous work. It is a matter of record that Santa Anna was cited for bravery for his participation in the Battle of Medina River in 1813, when the members of the Gutiérrez-Magee expedition, consisting largely of Americans, were summarily defeated. If he had not had previous military training, he was advancing fast for a teenager of seventeen. Parenthetically, his experience at Medina River bears out that he had begun to collect his ''debt'' against Americans.

According to Mrs. Reiner's version of the legend, Bull returned to Kentucky when his father Nathaniel died in 1826, ten years before the Battle of San Jacinto. He returned not to attend Nathaniel's funeral, or out of respect, but to demand his share of the Saunders' estate. By that time apparently the Saunders family had acquired considerable acreage. In substantiation of the family tradition, a barber in Gallatin County, Kentucky, who purchased some Saunders land, shortly before World War I, in Owen County (which had been carved out of Gallatin County in 1819), found—upon tracing the title—that the property had once belonged to General Santa Anna.

It is known that Santa Anna visited the United States on occasion. And by 1826 he was well on his way to political and military success. Certainly the opportunity to acquire wealth was in keeping with Santa Anna's character and addiction to luxury. For instance, his expensive tastes played the scale from monogrammed china to sterling silver receptacles and from silk underwear to diamond shirt studs valued at $1700 each.

Cobb's version of the tale, handed down by his grandfather, disclaims that Bull had any contact with his people after his disappearance. In fact, in this account Bull Saunders was not even heard of until after the Battle of San Jacinto in 1836.

This is understandable. If we may assume for a moment that any part of the legend is based on fact, then the metamorphosis from Bull Saunders to Santa Anna was complete by 1836. For nine years, following the Battle of Medina River, Santa Anna was busy constructing Indian villages, engaging in the prostitution of women, leading occasional military campaigns, and advancing to the rank of brigadier general. Then in 1822 he openly advocated Mexico's becoming a republic. In the interim, between 1822 and 1836, Santa Anna progressed from military governor of Yucatán to governor of Veracruz, suppressed the Spanish invasion of Tampico in 1829, and revolted against the Spanish government to step up to the presidency of Mexico—as a liberal—in 1833.

Next—reversing himself to become a dictator with centralist policies—Santa Anna crushed the Zacatecans in 1835 and prepared to force Texas under his totalitarian yoke in 1836. To complete the legendary assumption, Bull Saunders had ceased to exist. By 1836 he had risen to the prestige of a world figure heading his own empire. This position of power the dictator meant to retain at any cost—even at the risk of leading his own forces into the Mexican province of Texas. What did the ignoble Texans know about weapons and warfare beyond the shooting of long-eared jackrabbits and grinning racoons for pelts? And were not the settlers Americans like the sorry Kentuckians who had disowned him—"the Napoleon of the west?"

Cobb relates that for some reason not clear to the citizens of Frankfort the custody of Santa Anna—a prisoner of the Republic of Texas after the Battle of San Jacinto—was transferred to the United States government, and—the legend continues—that under a guard of dragoons, he traveled to the capital of the United States, where he obtained passage to Mexico on a naval vessel.

Though it is not generally believed that Santa Anna was placed in custody of the United States government after the Texas Revolution, history confirms that Sam Houston, then president of the Republic of Texas, personally arranged for the Mexican's trip to Washington, D. C., for an audience with President Andrew Jackson in October of 1836. History also verifies that the Mexican general and Colonel Juan N. Almonte were officially escorted to the national capitol by Inspector General of Texas George W. Hockley, William H. Patton, and Colonel Barnard E. Bee. It is also highly probable that Santa Anna was permitted to travel accompanied by his own escort of dragoons to serve him as personal aides. Records further confirm that the contingent traveled through Louisiana to the Mississippi River, then took a steamboat up that river to the Ohio, before proceeding to Kentucky.

Arriving in Kentucky—so the legend continues—Santa Anna and his guard took quarters in an inconspicuous tavern situated on the outskirts of town. It was not necessary that the Mexican and his entourage stop at Frankfort en route to Washington. But they did. Therefore tradition has it that Bull Saunders could not resist the urge to revisit the old familiar haunts of his boyhood days. To try to hide in an obscure and disreputable section of town, when he had been generously provided with a thousand dollars to fund the trip, indicated Santa Anna wished to avoid attracting attention.

Results of the Battle of San Jacinto and news of the Goliad massacre were well-known in Kentucky by October of 1836. Furthermore, news of Santa Anna's arrival in Frankfort spread over the town like a brush fire. Among the Kentuckians who had helped Texans win their independence were several volunteers from the immediate section of Frankfort, all of whom had been slaughtered with Colonel James W. Fannin at Goliad by Santa Anna's orders. History records that other Kentuckians had joined Sidney Sherman, a 30-year-old native of Massachusetts, who outfitted and financed a company of fifty-two volunteers who fought at San Jacinto. Sherman and his Kentucky volunteers had earned the reputation of being among the roughest and bravest fighters in the Texas army.

When they learned that Santa Anna was in town, a crowd of the dead soldiers' relatives and Kentucky patriots decided to lynch him for the cold-blooded murderer he was. Legend says they got some of the dragoons drunk and overpowered the rest. At the last minute, however, members of the mob changed their minds.

Why the patriotic Kentuckians altered their plan constitutes one of the most amazing legends relating to Texas and American history in circulation. Three men were selected to invade the tavern and deliver Santa Anna to the mob awaiting outside. When the delegation forced its way into Santa Anna's quarters, he was sitting up in bed. The leader turned out to be a kinsman—possibly a half-brother of Santa Anna or a first cousin—and both men recognized each other instantly. Immediately Santa Anna—so goes the legend—called out his Kentucky name and pled for mercy as a blood relative. He also professed to recognize the other two men as playmates of his boyhood spent in Forks of Elkhorn, where he had been born. The legend stresses that Santa Anna was an excellent supplicant.

Under a pledge of secrecy, Santa Anna was said to have told his would-be-lynchers a fabulous story. After escaping from West Point, he traveled to Mexico, mastered Spanish on the way, and twisted his English name around backward and shortened it to form *Santa Anna*. Thus he took *S a n* from his last name and reversed the *at* from the first to make *Santa*. Then he combined the *a n* and *N a* from the first to arrive at *Anna*. He ascribed to himself a fictitious birthplace and fabricated a family tree. He had exploited his excellent West Point training to rise to the highest rank in the Mexican army and, indeed, to the presidency. He rationalized his policy of giving no quarter and his butchery of his own countrymen at the Alamo and at Goliad on the grounds of military expediency. Once more he implored his former friends and his kinsman to spare his life.

The astonished Kentuckians were dissuaded from their original intent, not from compassion but because of the shame that would descend to their families and state if Bull Saunders' confession were revealed. Consequently, the delegation agreed to keep secret Santa Anna's incredible disclosures. They returned to the waiting mob and argued "that to hang a man under the protection of the United States flag" would involve not only the lynchmen but the state of Kentucky as well in a federal case. Convinced, the mob reluctantly disbanded.

The Mexican commander and his entourage proceeded to the national capital without further incident. In Washington Santa Anna, under Houston's instructions, assured President Jackson that Mexico would not try to reconquer Texas. Later, after being extensively wined and dined as a chief of state—not as a defeated commander—Santa Anna was given passage on the United States Navy frigate, the *Pioneer*, for his return to Mexico.

(Whether conversant with the legend or not, a Kentucky regiment captured Santa Anna's gold-fringed epaulets at Cerro Gordo, eleven years later, in 1847. At least an interesting sidelight is the fact that the battle trophy is on display in the State Museum at Frankfort.)

Dr. Reuben Saunders, an acknowledged nephew of the senior Nathaniel Saunders and Cobb's octogenarian grandfather, who related the tale to his seventeen-year-old grandson, declined to seek proof of the story that would have made him Santa Anna's first cousin. In fact, the story of his uncle's affair with the Cherokee squaw, he confided, was something the family avoided discussing. Still one member of each generation had violated the pledge of silence to pass the legend on before departing the scene.

Nor did Cobb make any effort to substantiate the underpinnings of the weird tale until many years later. When a newspaper assignment to cover the assassination of Kentucky Governor William Goebel—the political prototype of Louisiana's Huey P. Long—took Cobb to Frankfort in 1900, he tracked down an admission made by an ancient gentleman of the impossible name of Major Pat Major. Major had known personally members of the mob that surrounded the Frankfort tavern in 1836. Actually, though he would not concede it, the centenarian could have been the last surviving member of the mob. But a proud man, loyal to the traditions of Kentucky, he declined to give detail. His admission, however, excited the curiosity of Cobb—an investigative reporter—to seek additional evidence. In "a history of certain Blue Grass counties," Cobb states that he read that there was much confusion in

Frankfort upon Santa Anna's arrival that momentous day in October of 1836, and

> that after dark a disorderly and threatening assemblage with torches and weapons, trooped up the hill to listen to an impassioned harangue by one John U. Waring, a violent-minded orator, who subsequently died a violent death, but that it disbanded without offering any indignity to General Santa Anna . . .
> —Irvin S. Cobb, *Exit Laughing*, 37.

In checking deeper into Santa Anna's enigmatic history, Cobb discovered that Mexican authorities not only disagreed on the date and place of the dictator's birth but that Indians claimed he was "all Spanish by descent and the Spaniards insisted that he was all Indian." Furthermore, one biographer of the period intimated that Santa Anna had attended the great French cavalry school at St. Cyr, while another disproved it and attributed Santa Anna's expert military skill to the technical training he had received "in a famous governmental institution in the United States."

The Mexican general is buried in an infinitesimal and neglected plot at Amecameca, on a hilltop, overlooking the shrine of Our Lady of Guadalupe, in Mexico City. Santa Anna's monument bears the simple inscription: *"El Presidente Antonio López de Santa Anna, 1795-1876."*

Should the epitaph read: *"El Toro de Saunders, hijo ilegítimo del Señor Nathaniel Saunders y fugitivo de West Point, 1795-1876"*?

Sam Houston

SAM HOUSTON, CIRCA 1862. ENGRAVING BY H. B. HALL & SONS, NEW YORK, FROM A DAGUERREOTYPE, COURTESY THE NEW YORK PUBLIC LIBRARY.

Sam Houston

ONE of the most controversial and dramatic names in American history is that of Sam Houston. While Houston's critics remain adamant, his venerators are equally loyal. In the one hundred thirteen years since his death, more than a hundred books about him have been published, including one by the author—*Sam Houston And His Twelve Women.*

Different states claim Houston: Virginia, where he was born on Texas Independence Day, March 2, 1793; Tennessee, where he was elected to the United States Congress in 1823 and 1825, to the governorship in 1827, and was married to Eliza Allen, his first wife, January 1, 1829; Arkansas, where he became a Cherokee citizen on November 29, 1829, and took his second wife, Tiana Rogers.

But the state with which Houston best identifies is Texas. For more than two decades he dominated the Texas political scene. He served the Republic of Texas as its first president, from 1836 to 1838, and its third, from 1841 to 1844. Houston was governor of Texas from 1859 to 1861, served intermittently in the state legislature, and represented Texas in the United States Senate for almost fourteen years.

The son of Samuel and Elizabeth (Paxton) Houston, pioneer settlers of Rockbridge County, Virginia, Houston was both a self-made and self-taught man. Living among the Cherokees before migrating to Texas in 1832, he immersed himself in the classics of two cultures: the traditions of religious mysticism and books of the humanities, invariably among them his favorite copy of the *Iliad*. Some historians believe Houston came to Texas on a mission for Andrew Jackson to negotiate with the Comanche Indians of San Antonio. Others theorize that, as Jackson's emissary, Houston migrated to the Mexican province to pursue a more significant and long-range objective. In view of this premise, it is interesting to note that President Jackson's last official act, before leaving office, was to sign into law on March 3, 1837, the bill that recognized the autonomy of the Republic of Texas.

Sam Houston marched to the tempo of a different drum. The protegé of Jackson, who groomed him well for destiny's role, Houston was a man of caution who liked to win, whether on the battlefield or in the political arena. The major defeat of his career was his inability to prevent Texas from seceding and joining the Confederacy since he believed that the South could not win the Civil War. He took the failure in stride, nonetheless, just as he bore his battle scars stoically to the end of his life. The body wound inflicted by the Indian arrow at Horseshoe Bend. The injured ankle that stopped a Mexican *escopeta* ball at San Jacinto. Houston sustained another crushing defeat when his namesake Sam, fighting for the South, was wounded at Shiloh.

Houston married his third wife, Margaret Lea of Marion, Alabama, May 9, 1840. Despite the age difference (he was 47 and she was 22), the marriage was successful. The couple had eight children, all of whom made notable contributions to their time. After being deposed from the Texas governorship in 1861, for declining to pledge allegiance to the Confederacy, Houston and his wife retired to their home in Huntsville, where he died on July 26, 1863, and is buried.

Monuments to Sam Houston extend from Texas to Washington, D.C. However, the one he probably would prefer stands at the entrance of his favorite home and shrine in Huntsville, across from the campus of the university named for him—the immense pecan tree that has borne fruit since he planted it as a sapling in 1847.

Bibliographic Notes

PROLOGUE

[1]Jan Harold Brunvand, *The Study of American Folklore* (New York, 1969), 130.

[2]*Ibid.*, 131.

[3]*Ibid.*, 131-132.

[4]This is the deduction of the writer after making a careful scrutiny of a score of variants of "The Yellow Rose of Texas."

[5]Edwin W. Gaston, Jr., "Martha Anne Turner, *The Yellow Rose of Texas*," Review in *The South Central Bulletin*, Vol. XXXII, No. 2 (May, 1972), 57.

CHAPTER ONE
Santa Anna and The Slave Girl at San Jacinto

[1]R. Henderson Shuffler, "San Jacinto, As She Was Or, What Really Happened On The Plain of St. Hyacinth On A Hot April Afternoon in 1836," Typescript furnished the author. See also Frank X. Tolbert, *The Day of San Jacinto* (New York, 1962), 76.

[2]The Honorable Thomas J. Stovall, Jr., Judge One Hundred Twenty-Ninth District of Texas, to Martha Anne Turner, November 7, 1973. Judge Stovall, a founder of the organization known as the "Sons of the Knights of the Yellow Rose of Texas" (SKYRT), asserts that, in addition to the United States, membership has spread over much of the world, including the Province of

British Columbia, the Virgin Islands, Puerto Rico, Hawaii, and Mexico. He says that it is impossible "to walk through any international airport without spotting one of our members carrying a briefcase. In fact, we are everywhere." Members are identified by a small yellow rose "embroidered impeccably upon a base of velcroz" attached to their lapels.

[3] Andrew Forest Muir, "The Free Negro in Harris County, Texas," *Southwestern Historical Quarterly*, XLVI (July, 1942-April, 1943), 218.

[4] *Ibid*. See also Harold Schoen, "The Free Negro in The Republic of Texas," *Southwestern Historical Quarterly*, XXXIX (July, 1935-April, 1936), 299-308.

[5] Walter Prescott Webb and others (eds.), *The Handbook of Texas* (2 Vols.; Austin, 1952), II, 234.

[6] *Ibid.*

[7] James K. Morgan, Morgan Papers, Rosenberg Library, Galveston, Texas.

[8] *Ibid.*

[9] *Ibid.*

[10] Muir, "The Free Negro in Harris County, Texas," *Southwestern Historical Quarterly*, XLVI (July, 1942-April, 1943), 219. See also Schoen, "The Free Negro in The Republic of Texas," *Southwestern Historical Quarterly*, XXXIX (July, 1935-April, 1936), 299-308.

[11] *Passports, 1836-1844: Letter Book of the Department of State* (MSS, in Archives, Texas State Library, Austin), II, 47-48.

[12] Lucy A. Erath (ed.), *Memoirs of George Bernard Erath* (Austin, 1923), 40-48.

[13] George Sessions Perry, *Texas: A World in Itself* (New York, 1941), 207. See also Martha Anne Turner, *William Barret Travis: His Sword And His Pen* (Waco, 1972), 98-99.

[14] Eugene C. Barker, *The Life of Stephen F. Austin* (Austin, 1949), 184.

[15]Carlos E. Castañeda, *The Mexican Side of The Texas Revolution* (Dallas, 1928), 74-75. See also Llerena Friend, *Sam Houston: The Great Designer* (Austin, 1954), 68-69, and M. K. Wisehart, *Sam Houston: American Giant* (Washington, D. C., 1962), 226.

[16]Colonel Pedro Delgado, "Mexican Account of The Battle of San Jacinto," *The Texas Almanac: 1857-1873* (Waco, 1967), 614. See also Colonel Pedro Delgado, "The Battle of San Jacinto. . . An Account of the Action Written by Colonel Pedro Delgado of General Santa Anna's Staff," William Carey Crane, *Life and Select Remains of Sam Houston of Texas* (Philadelphia, 1885), 648-661.

[17]Henderson Yoakum, *History of Texas From Its Settlement in 1685 To Its Annexation To The United States in 1846* (2 Vols.; New York, 1859), II, 36ff. See also Tolbert, *The Day of San Jacinto*, 72-73.

[18]Delgado, "Mexican Account of The Battle of San Jacinto," *The Texas Almanac: 1857-1873*, 615. See also translation in Crane, *Life and Select Remains of Sam Houston of Texas*, as cited above, 648-661.

[19]Wisehart, *Sam Houston: American Giant*, 227. See also Delgado's account as previously cited.

[20]"Compendium of The History of Texas (Continued from the *Texas Almanac* for 1859)," *The Texas Almanac: 1857-1873*, 332. See also Eugene C. Barker, *History of Texas* (Dallas, 1929), 233ff and Carlos E. Castaneda, *Our Catholic Heritage* (6 Vols.; Austin, 1950), VI, 257-281.

[21]"Compendium of The History of Texas . . . ," *The Texas Almanac: 1857-1873*, 332.

[22]*Ibid*. See also Castañeda, *The Mexican Side of The Texas Revolution* as cited above.

[23]*Ibid*.

[24]Wisehart, *Sam Houston: American Giant*, 227. See also Tolbert, *The Day of San Jacinto*, 78-79.

[25]Delgado, "Mexican Account of The Battle of San Jacinto," *The Texas Almanac: 1857-1873*, 615.

[26]*Ibid*. See also Wisehart, *Sam Houston: American Giant*, 227-228.

[27]*Ibid*.

[28]Delgado, "Mexican Account of The Battle of San Jacinto," *The Texas Almanac: 1857-1873*, 615.

[29]Anthony Menchaca, *Anthony Menchaca Papers*, San Antonio Public Library, San Antonio, Texas. See also Tolbert, *The Day of San Jacinto*, 24-25.

[30]General Vicente Filisola, *Memorias Para La Historia de La Guerra de Tejas* (Mexico: Ignacio Cumplido, 1849), II, 212. For related material from the Mexican point of view, see also Antonio Lopez de Santa Anna to the Minister of War and Marine, October 26, 1835. University of Texas transcripts, Guerra, Fraccion, 1, Exp. 10 (Operaciones Militares, 1835: Texas), *passim*.

[31]For a detailed account of the celebrated Forbes Case see Martha Anne Turner, *Texas Epic: An American Story*, Document Number 11.

[32]Delgado, "Mexican Account of the Battle of San Jacinto," *The Texas Almanac: 1857-1873*, 617. For related material see also Castañeda and Filisola as previously cited.

[33]Wisehart, *Sam Houston: American Giant*, 225.

[34]Tolbert, *The Day of San Jacinto*, 116.

[35]Lota M. Spell, *Music in Texas* (Austin, 1936), 34. See also Webb and others (eds.), *The Handbook of Texas*, I, 968-969.

[36]Spell, *Music in Texas*, 27.

[37]*Ibid*, 107.

[38]Marquis James, *The Raven* (New York, 1929), 247. See also Friend, *Sam Houston: The Great Designer*, 267.

³⁹Dr. N. D. Labadie, "San Jacinto Campaign," *The Texas Almanac: 1857-1873*, 159. See also Delgado, "The Mexican Side of the Texas Revolution," *The Texas Almanac . . .* , 613ff.

⁴⁰L. W. Kemp and Ed Kilman, "The Battle of San Jacinto And The San Jacinto Campaign," (a brochure, 1947), 11. See also Tolbert, *The Day of San Jacinto*, 118-119; Moses Austin Bryan, "Lamar at San Jacinto," *The Texas Almanac . . .* , 674-675.

⁴¹*Ibid.*

⁴²Dr. Labadie, "San Jacinto Campaign," *The Texas Almanac . . .* , 159-160.

⁴³Tolbert, *The Day of San Jacinto*, 130.

⁴⁴*Ibid.*

⁴⁵*Ibid.*, 127.

⁴⁶Claude Garner, *Sam Houston: Texas Giant* (San Antonio, 1969), 251.

⁴⁷Richard G. Santos, *Santa Anna's Campaign Against Texas: 1835-1836* (Waco, 1968), 99.

⁴⁸Delgado, "Mexican Account of the Battle of San Jacinto," *The Texas Almanac: 1857-1873*, 617. See also Castaneda and Felisola as previously cited.

⁴⁹Wisehart, *Sam Houston: American Giant*, 218-219.

⁵⁰Tolbert, *The Day of San Jacinto*, 130.

⁵¹*Ibid.*, 166. See also Yoakum, *History of Texas . . .* , II, 103.

⁵²Tolbert, *The Day of San Jacinto*, 130-131.

⁵³Most authorities place the official figure at 1568, including Marquis James (*The Raven*, 252) and Houston himself in his official report.

⁵⁴Garner, *Sam Houston: Texas Giant*, 221.

⁵⁵*Ibid.*

⁵⁶Amelia Williams and Eugene C. Barker (eds.), *The Writings of Sam Houston* (8 Vols.; Austin, 1938-1943), V, 173-175; VI, 5-13, 184-191, 448-461; VII, 306-336, 325-326. Houston himself remains the best reference on details of the preparations for the Battle of San Jacinto.

⁵⁷Walter Lord, *A Time To Stand* (New York, 1951), 195.

⁵⁸Wisehart, *Sam Houston: American Giant*, 239-240. See also Tolbert, *The Day of San Jacinto*, 140ff.

⁵⁹Santos, *Santa Anna's Campaign Against Texas: 1835-1836*, 99. There is no disagreement on this point.

⁶⁰Kemp and Kilman, "The Battle of San Jacinto And The San Jacinto Campaign," (a brochure, 1947), *passim*. See also Dr. Labadie, "San Jacinto Campaign," *The Texas Almanac...*, 163ff.

⁶¹Sam Houston, Commander in Chief, to David G. Burnet, President of the Republic of Texas, headquarters of the Army, San Jacinto, April 25, 1836, Yoakum, *History of Texas...*, Appendix, II, 501. See also *The Writings of Sam Houston*, I, 416-420.

⁶²Lois Foster Blount, "A Brief Study of Thomas Jefferson Rusk Based on His Letters to His Brother, David, 1835-1856," *Southwestern Historical Quarterly*, XXXIV (1930-1931), 279ff. See also Thomas J. Rusk, *Rusk Papers*, Archives, University of Texas at Austin; Colonel Robert M. Coleman, *Houston Displayed Or Who Won The Battle of San Jacinto* (Austin, 1964, reprint), 27-28; "Thomas Jefferson Rusk," *The Texas Almanac...*, 62.

⁶³*Ibid*.

⁶⁴*Ibid*. See also James, *The Raven*, 246ff. Later after Houston went to New Orleans for surgery his wound was diagnosed "'as a compound fracture of the right tibia and fibula, just above the ankle ... Years later Houston's son, Colonel Andrew Houston, said it was 'a copper ball from a Mexican escopeta'."—Tolbert, *The Day of San Jacinto*, 168.

⁶⁵Andrew Forest Muir, "The Mystery of San Jacinto," *Southwest Review* 36 (1951), 83. See also H. M. Henderson,

"A Critical Analysis of the San Jacinto Campaign," *Southwestern Historical Quarterly*, LIX (April, 1955 - April, 1956), 360; Tolbert, *The Day of San Jacinto*, 108; and Sam Houston Dixon and Louis Wiltz Kemp, *The Heroes of San Jacinto* (Houston, 1932), 100-101.

[66]Henderson, "A Critical Analysis of the San Jacinto Campaign," *Southwestern Historical Quarterly*, LIX (April, 1955 - April, 1956), 114. See also Muir, "The Mystery of San Jacinto," *Southwest Review*, 36 (1951), 77-84.

[67]Henderson, "A Critical Analysis of the San Jacinto Campaign," *Southwestern Historical Quarterly*, LIX (April, 1955-April, 1956), 114. See also Webb and others (eds.), *The Handbook of Texas*, II, 24-25.

[68]Tolbert, *The Day of San Jacinto*, 141.

[69]This is the version of "Will You Come To The Bower?" as it appears in *Amateur's Songbook* and various standard anthologies.

[70]Ethel Chauncey O. Moore (collector), *Ballads and Folk Songs of The Southwest* (Norman, Oklahoma, 1964), 212.

[71]Williams and Barker (eds.), *The Writings of Sam Houston*, I, 416-420. See also Yoakum, *History of Texas* . . . , Appendix, II, 501.

[72]*Ibid.*, 500.

[73]Thomas J. Rusk, Secretary of War, to David G. Burnet, President of Texas, War Department, Headquarters, Army of Texas, San Jacinto, April 22, 1836, Yoakum, *History of Texas* . . . , II, 504.

[74]James, *The Raven*, 252. See also "List of All The Men at The Battle of San Jacinto," *The Texas Almanac* . . . , 237.

[75]*Ibid*. In his report to Burnet Houston gives the number of Texans wounded as 23 evidently excluding himself—Yoakum, *History of Texas* . . . , 501.

[76]Delgado, "The Battle of San Jacinto . . . An Account of the Action Written by Colonel Pedro Delgado of General Santa

Anna's Staff," Crane, *Life and Select Remains of Sam Houston of Texas*, 648-661. See also Ramon Caro, *Verdadera Idea de la Primera Campana de Tejas, passim*, and Filisola and Castañeda as previously cited.

[77]*Ibid*. See also Tolbert, *The Day of San Jacinto*, 174-175.

[78]*Ibid*.

[79]*Ibid*.

[80]Lucy A. Erath (ed.), *Memoirs of George Bernard Erath*, 40-48.

[81]*Ibid*.

[82]"Joel Walter Robison's Account of the Capture of Santa Anna," *The Texas Almanac...*, 243. See also Yoakum, *History of Texas...*, II, 146.

[83]*Ibid*. See also Wisehart, *Sam Houston: American Giant*, 247.

[84]Clarence R. Wharton, *Life of General Santa Anna: El Presidente...* (Austin, 1926), 59.

[85]*Ibid*. See also "Joel Walter Robison's Account of the Capture of Santa Anna," *The Texas Almanac...*, 243ff, and Tolbert, *The Day of San Jacinto*, 175.

[86]Ann Fears Crawford (ed.), *The Eagle: The Autobiography of Santa Anna* (Austin, 1967), 265ff.

[87]Williams and Barker (eds.), *The Writings of Sam Houston*, I, 435. See also Charles Edward Lester, *The Life of Sam Houston: The Only Authentic Memoir of Him Ever Published* (New York, 1855), 144-145.

[88]Wilfred Hardy Callcott, *Santa Anna: The Story of An Enigma Who Once Was Mexico* (Norman, Oklahoma, 1936), 139. See also Wharton, *Life of General Santa Anna...*, 25.

[89]Wisehart, *Sam Houston: American Giant*, 250-251. See also Wharton, *Life of General Santa Anna: El Presidente...*, 60.

[90]For texts of both Treaties of Velasco and "Ratification of the Public Agreement by Filisola . . . ," see Yoakum, *History of Texas* . . . , II, 526-530.

[91]Had Emily not survived the battle, she could not have related her experience to Colonel Morgan verbatim as William Bollaert asserts. See W. Eugene Holland and Ruth Lapham Butler (eds.), *William Bollaert's Texas* (Norman, Oklahoma, 1956), 108n.

[92]*Passports, 1836-1844: Letter Book of the Department of State* (MSS. in Archives, Texas State Library, Austin), II, 47-48. See also Muir, "The Free Negro in Harris County, Texas," as previously cited.

[93]Tolbert, *The Day of San Jacinto*, 199.

[94]*Ibid*. There is no disagreement on this point.

[95]See *Passports, 1836-1844*, as previously cited.

[96]Crawford (ed.), *The Eagle: The Autobiography of Santa Anna*, 265. See also *Morgan Papers* as previously cited.

[97]Hollon and Butler (eds.), *William Bollaert's Texas*, 108n.

[98]According to Ann Fears Crawford, Mexican historians generally have verified the incident involving Emily and their first informant was Santa Anna himself—Crawford (ed.), *The Eagle: The Autobiography of Santa Anna*, 265.

[99]*Ibid*. See also Shuffler, "San Jacinto, As She Was: Or What Really Happened On The Plain of St. Hyacinth On A Hot April Afternoon In 1836," Francis Edward Abernethy (ed.), *Observations & Reflections On Texas Folklore* (Austin, 1972), 123.

[100]Donald Day and Harry Herbert Ullom, *The Autobiography of Sam Houston* (Norman, Oklahoma, 1954), xii. See also Webb and others (eds.), *The Handbook of Texas*, II, 554, and John A. Garraty, *The American Nation, passim*.

[101]"Present plans include a memorial ceremony to be held at the spot where our County Surveyor has indicated President-General Antonio López de Santa Anna y Perez de Lebron's tent

was located to erect a suitable monument in honor of Emily. At the very time the Governor of Texas is reviewing the Texas Navy from the deck of the *Sam Houston*, just astern of the *Battleship Texas*, we have engaged the services of a handsome schooner launched in 1891 named *The Trumpeter*. We have two bronze cannon said to be exact replicas of the Twin Sisters and we are to establish a beachhead at Peggy's Lake and storm the heights with our monument carefully wrapped in a tote-sack. A small group of boy scouts from the City of Pasadena has agreed to dress themselves in Mexican uniforms and provide brisk opposition to our landing"—The Honorable Thomas J. Stovall, Jr., to Martha Anne Turner, November 7, 1973.

CHAPTER TWO

Manuscript Copy of The Folksong

[1] J. L. Clark, *A History of Texas: Land of Promise* (Boston, 1939), 275. See also Donald Day and Harry Herbert Ullom, *The Autobiography of Sam Houston* (Norman, 1954), 137-138.

[2] *Journal of the Proceedings of the General Council of the Republic of Texas at San Felipe de Austin from March 14, 1835, to March 1, 1836; Ordinances and Decrees of the Provisional Government* (1838), Archives, Texas State Library, Austin.

[3] H. P. N. Gammel (ed.), *Laws of Texas*, I, II, (Austin, 1898), *passim*. See also W. L. Newson, "The Postal System of the Republic of Texas," *Southwestern Historical Quarterly*, XX (1916-1917), 103-131.

[4] *Ibid*. See also Webb and others (eds.), *The Handbook of Texas*, II, 399.

[5] All sources agree on this point. Houston and other officials continued this practice of transmitting mail by courier, particularly important or official messages, throughout his second term as president of the Republic of Texas.

[6] Howard Mumford Jones, *The Harp That Once—* (New York, 1937), 65. See also *Tom Moore's Diary*, with an Introduction by J. B. Priestly (Cambridge, 1925), 134-135.

⁷Frank X. Tolbert, *An Informal History of Texas* (New York, 1951), 92. See also Colonel James Morgan, *Morgan Papers*, Rosenberg Library, Galveston.

⁸The text follows that of a handwritten copy in the *A. Henry Moss Papers*, Archives Collection, The University of Texas Library, Austin.

CHAPTER THREE

First Copyright Edition of The Song

¹Copyright Records, the Library of Congress, Washington, D. C. See also James J. Fuld, *The Book of World Famous Music* . . . (New York, 1971), 661.

²*Ibid.*

³A. Pat Daniels, *Texas Avenue at Main Street* (Houston, 1964), 8-9.

⁴John Harrington Cox (ed.), *Folk-Songs of The South* (Cambridge, 1925), 396.

⁵*Ibid.*

⁶"The Yellow Rose of Texas," original first edition in the Archives of The University of Texas, Austin, Texas.

CHAPTER FOUR

A Civil War Marching Song

¹Walter Prescott Webb and others (eds.), *The Handbook of Texas*, II, 946. Mrs. Young was named official mother of Hood's Texas Brigade and, because of her deep interest in the Civil War and the South's participation, she also became known as the "Confederate Lady."

²John Spencer Bassett, *A Short History of the United States* (New York, 1929), 537-539. See also, Richard N. Current and others, *American History: A Survey* (New York, 1961), 425-426. When the Confederate general Joseph E. Johnston fell

back to Atlanta before the march of Sherman, he incurred sharp criticism and was replaced by General John B. Hood. In eleven days the aggressive Hood lost three battles. Then as a threat to Sherman's base at Atlanta, he detoured westward to Decatur, Alabama, on the Tennessee River—110 miles south of Nashville. He had acted on the premise that the Union leader would hasten back to that city.

But he underestimated Sherman, who sent General Thomas to Nashville reinforced by 60,000 veteran fighters. Sherman followed Hood until the Confederate general tipped his hand by crossing the Tennessee River on October 20, 1864. At this point the Union officer concentrated an additional 60,000 seasoned troops at Atlanta to hold the city. Meanwhile Hood's men became disgruntled at his losses and regretted the removal of their former general. This fact, coupled with Hood's three-week delay to collect supplies, spelled out his defeat. Unable to move until November 21, the Confederate general was delayed by Schofield's force of 29,000 men. When Schofield intrenched at Franklin to repair the bridge on the Harpeth River, Hood attacked. The move was disastrous.

From four o'clock in the afternoon until dark, the Yankees slashed their way to victory, then proceeded to Nashville, only twenty miles away. Whereas Union losses were 2,326 men, Confederate casualties ran to 6,000. With his forces reduced to 23,000 Hood encamped in the hills south of the city.

Already occupying Nashville, General Thomas, a cautious fighter, did not attack Hood until December 15. After two days of intense fighting, the Confederates were forced to retreat, totally demoralized. When they crossed the Tennessee River on December 27, their number had been reduced to fewer than 15,000 cavalrymen. As a result, the soldiers added their own lyrical commentary to the song. While the Southern soldiers concurred that their aggressive leader was brave, they charged him with full responsibility for their decisive defeat.

[3] J. Frank Dobie, with an Introduction by Bertha Dobie, *Carl Sandburg & Saint Peter At The Gate* (Austin, 1966), *passim*. See also Karl W. Deitzer, *Carl Sandburg: A Study in Personality and Background* (New York, 1941).

CHAPTER SEVEN

Transcriptions by David W. Guion

[1]Charles J. Finger, "A Note On Texas," *Southwesterners Write* (New Mexico, 1947), 8-9.

[2]David W. Guion to Martha Anne Turner, October 15, 1970.

[3]David W. Guion to Martha Anne Turner, November 18, 1970.

CHAPTER EIGHT

"The Yellow Rose of Texas" in World War II

[1]Numerous songbooks verify the statement.

[2]Hugo Frey (ed.), *Victory Song Book for Soldiers, Sailors and Marines* (New York, 1942), 73.

[3]John Mayfield, prothokeeper of The Mayfield Library of Texas, Maryland, New York, to Martha Anne Turner, January 11, 1972.

Index

Aguirre, Captain Miguel: 16
Alamo: 12, 14, 23, 24, 108
Allen, Eliza: first wife of Houston, 13
Almanac 1857-1873, The Texas: quoted from, 24
Almonte, Colonel Juan N.: 31, 34, 105
Amateur's Songbook: 26
Amecameca: 110
America: 49, 67
Americana: 86
American bicentennial: xii
American Revolution: 99
Americans: 8, 34, 101, 105
American serviceman: xii, 82
American Studies Association of Texas: xiii
American tradition: xiv, 79, 95
Antone, Dr. E. H.: xiv
Arnold, Hendrick: 25, 35
Austin, San Felipe de: 41
Austin, Stephen F.: 7, 16

Bachiller, Miguel: Filisola's conduit, 20
"Ballads and Folksongs of The Southwest": 27
Barker Texas History Center: 52
Barragan, Captain Marcos: 10-11, 15
Barrera, Melchora Iniega: 12
Baylor University: 78
Bee, Colonel Barnard E.: 105
Beebe, John: 25
Bennett, Clois: 52
Bennett, Lieutenant Colonel Joseph: 22
Bermuda: Negroes from, 6, 46
Bexar: 41

Blakely, Private Lemuel Stockton: 30
Blue Grass Counties: 109
Boatright, Mody C.: xiv
Bollaert, William: quoted, 37; Papers, 37; *William Bollaert's Texas*, 37
Bostick, Private S. R.: 31, 33
Brazos River: 20, 32
Briscoe, Janey: viii
Brown, Charles H.: 49, 51
Bryan, Moses Austin: 34
Buffalo Bayou: 13, 19, 25
Burleson, Colonel Edward: 31
Burnet, *ad interim* President David G.: 9, 30
Bust, Luke: 25
Butler, Ruth Lapham: 37

cannon: 16, 19; Santa Anna's fieldpiece — the *Gold Standard*, 13, 14; Houston's two pieces — the *Twin Sisters*, 14, 15
Cantonment Jessup: 44
Castrillón, General Manuel Fernández: 13, 19, 31
Cayuga (ship): 35
Cerro Gordo, Battle of: 109
chamberpot: Santa Anna's mounted sterling, 7
champagne: 12, 18, 19, 31
Cherokees: 113, 114; Cherokee squaw, 109
Christy's Minstrels: 49
Civil War: "The Yellow Rose of Texas" in, 53-54; mentioned, 25, 65, 114; "Ballads and Folksongs of the," 53

131

Coahuila-Texas: 8
Cobb, Irvin S.: quoted, 110; see also Santa Anna Legend, The, 99-111
Collins, Richard: 100
Columbia Records: 87
Comanche Indians: 114
Confederacy, the: 53-54, 114, 115
Confederate soldiers: 52, 92
Cos, General Martín Perfecto de: 19, 20, 31, 34
Crawford, Ann Fears: 102

George, Don: 2, 3, 87
"Girl I Left Behind, The": see music at San Jacinto
Goebel, Governor William: 109
Gold Standard, The: see cannon
Goliad: 23; massacre of, 24, 106, 108
Gonzales: 12
Greenwich Village: 68
Guadalupe River: 12
Guion, David W.: transcriptions by, 67-78; mentioned, 2, 55, 87
Gutiérrez-Magee expedition: 103

Daughters of the Confederacy Museum: 65
"Deguello:" 4
Delgado, Colonel Pedro: 11; quoted, 13-14; engages Texans in action, 15, 19, 31
Dell Book of Great American Folk Songs, The: 53, 54
Dobie, J. Frank: xiv, 54
dragoons: 8, 10, 12, 16, 17, 19, 105, 106, 107
Dressler, William: 55

Eagle, The: 102
Erath, George Bernard: discovers evidence of Santa Anna's dissipation, 31
Exit Laughing: 99; quoted from, 99-110

Fannin, Colonel James W.: 106
Filisola, General Vicente: 20, 21, 32
folklore: 37, 66
Forbes, Commissioner-General John: 12
Forks of Elkhorn, Kentucky: 99, 107
Frankfort, Kentucky: 99, 100, 105
Frey, Hugo: 79, 81, 93, 94

Galveston: 5, 6, 8, 9, 35

Haring, Robert C.: 85
Harrisburg: 8, 15, 16, 31
Hatcher, Mattie Austin: 65
H. B. C.: 44
Hertzog, Carl: xiv
Hill Country: xii
History of Kentucky: 99
Hockley, George W.: 105
Holley, Mary Austin: 16
Hollon, W. Eugene: 37
Hood, General John B.: 53, 54-55
Horseshoe Bend, Battle of: 114
Houston, Elizabeth (Paxton): 114
Houston, Sam (son): 114-115
Houston, General Sam: position of, 10; pickets of, 13; gets bridle clipped, 15; and Sidney Sherman, 16; reprimands Sherman and promotes Lamar, 18; views insubordination, 18-19; learns of Mexican reinforcements, 20; remains circumspect, 20; orders destruction of Vince's bridge, 20-21; orders Smith to ascertain enemy strength, 21; receives Smith's report, 21-22; aware of Emily in Santa Anna's tent, 22; prepares for battle, 22; gives charge to attack, 22-23; sustains ankle injury, 24; tries to restore discipline, 34-35; replaced by Rusk, 35; and battle music, 25-29; releases battle statistics, 29-30; receives Santa Anna as

prisoner of war, 34; biographical sketch of, 113-116 *passim*; first administration, 41; mentioned, 44, 45, 105
Houston, Samuel (father): 114
Hudson River: 101
Hunter, Private Bob: quoted, 24
Huntsville, Texas: 115

Iturbide, Augustín de: 7

Jackson, President Andrew: Houston's patron, 20, 114; last official act of, 114; as host to Santa Anna, 105-108
Jackson, Tennessee: 49
"J. K.": 49, 51, 55, 85, 86, 87
Johnson, Lyndon Baines: xii
"Jones, E. A.": 41
Jones, John Rice: 41

Kentucky: state of, 99, 102, 106, 107; patriots of, 106, 107; see also Santa Anna Legend, The
Kleberg, Robert Justus: 16

Labadie, Dr. N. D.: 24
Lamar, Mirabeau B.: in skirmish for cannon, 16-17; shoots Mexican lancer, 17, 22
Lamb, Second Lieutenant George A.: 30
Lane, Walter P.: 16-17, 21, 25
Lea, Margaret: third wife of Houston, 115
Lemsky, Frederick: 25
Lenz, Louis: 52
Long, Huey P.: 109
Louisville *Courier Journal*: 99
Lynchburg ferry: 32
Lynchburg, Texas: 10
Lynch's Ferry: 11

Major, Major Pat: 109
Marion, Alabama: 115
marquee: description of, 7; set up at San Jacinto, 14, 20; purchased by Morgan, 35-36
Masonic Lodge: 34
Masonic distress signal: 34
Massachusetts: 106
McCullough, Casey: viii
medallion: see Yellow Rose, The
Medina River, Battle of: 103
Menifee, Private John S.: quoted, 25-26
Mexican army: 5, 8, 9, 10, 11, 12, 13, 23, 30, 108
Mexican cannoneers: 14
Mexican reinforcements: 20
Mexican War: 25, 34
Mexico: 7, 8; Interior Provinces of, 102-103, 104, 105
Mexico City: 12, 110
Miles, Private Alfred: 31, 33
Miller, Mitch: 2, 3; see also Mitch Miller Adaptation, The, 87-92 *passim*
Mississippi River: 106
Monterrey: 38
Moore, Thomas: composer of "Will You Come to The Bower?", 25, 26, 46
Morgan, Colonel James: patriot and colonizer, 5-6; family of, 5; plantation, 6, 8-9, 35
Morgan, Emily: inspires medallion, viii; inspires song, xii, 41, 95; description of, 5; "The Yellow Rose of Texas," an international legend, 5; and Santa Anna, 5, 22; and Sam Houston, vii; background of, 5-6; and Colonel Morgan, 5-6; captured by Santa Anna, 9-10; en route to San Jacinto, 13; and yellow boy Turner, 9-10; as replacement for Melchora Iniega Barrera, 12; arrives at San Jacinto, 14; with Santa Anna at San Jacinto, 15-16; as "guest" in rococo quarters, 19-20; presence known to Houston, 21; serves Santa Anna breakfast, 22; parties with Santa Anna, 22;

133

survives Battle of San Jacinto, 34-35; relates experience to Colonel Morgan, 35; granted freedom, 35; story of, passed on to Bollaert, 36; quoted indirectly by Bollaert, 37; reasons for censorship of, 36-38; story of, circulated as legend, 37; verification of, by Mexican historians, 37-38; as Santa Anna's "quadroon mistress," 37; the question of infatuation with Santa Anna, 38; the question of loyalty to Texas, 38; value of contribution, 38-39; as "Emily, the maid of Morgan's Point," 45; perpetuation through "Sons of the Knights of the Yellow Rose of Texas (SKYRT)," 39; as heroine of Texas Revolution, 95; see also San Jacinto, Battle of, and Santa Anna, Antonio López de

Morgan's Point: 5, 35; see also New Washington
Morse, Jim: 34
Moss, A. Henry: Papers, 41, 79
Motley, Dr. William Junius: 30
mules: 10, 12, 15
Munich: xiii
music at San Jacinto: performers, 25; reasons for choice of, 26; text of "Will You Come to The Bower?", 27; text of "The Girl I Left Behind," 28-29

"Napoleon of the West": See Santa Anna, Antonio López de
Negro folk music: 2, 55, 93
Neill, Lieutenant Colonel James: 15
New Orleans: 44
New Spain: Interior Provinces of, 102-103
New Washington: 6, 9-10, 15, 18, 21, 30, 35, 36, 46
New York: 5, 6, 35, 36, 49, 93

Ohio River: 106
Old Whip: Santa Anna escapes on, 30, 32

O. Moore, Ethel Chauncey: 27
opium: see Santa Anna, Antonio López de

Patton, William H.: 105
pecan tree: planted by Houston, 115
Pedernales River: xii
Philadelphia: 6
piano/pianos: 8, 15-16, 85
Pioneer (ship): 108
Pond, William A. & Company: 49, 55
postal system: of Republic of Texas, 41, 44

"quadroon mistress": see Morgan, Emily

Reiner, Mrs. Martha (Sanders): see Santa Anna Legend, The
Riley, Claude T.: viii
Rio Grande River: 91
Robison, Joel: 32, 33, 34
Rockbridge, Virginia: 114
Rogers, Tiana: second wife of Houston, 113
Roosevelt, Franklin Delano: dedication of "The Yellow Rose of Texas" to, 68; and David W. Guion, 77
"Rose": as song symbol, 45; "Hateful rose," annotation of first copyright edition, 52, 64
Round-Up Memories: 85, 86
Rusk, Secretary of War Thomas: 16; rescued by Lamar, 17; endorses promotion of Lamar, 18; replaces Houston at San Jacinto, 24; takes prisoners, 24; helps to preserve Santa Anna's life, 34; mentioned, 36, 44

Saipan, Island of: 82
Sam Houston State University: xiv
San Antonio: viii, 11, 12, 114

Sandburg, Carl: quoted, 54
Sanders: see Saunders
San Jacinto, Battle of: 5-40 *passim*. See also Houston, Sam; Morgan, Emily, and Santa Anna, Antonio López de
San Jacinto Bay: 14, 19, 20, 39
San Jacinto River: 5, 19, 21
Santa Anna, General Antonio López de: as part of international legend, 5; character and description of, 6-7; rise to power, 7-8; at Harrisburg, 8; pursues government officials, 8-9; at New Washington, 8-9; captures Emily and Turner, 8-10; panics at news of Houston's approach, 10-11; addiction to opium, 11, 34; mock marriage in San Antonio, 11-12; en route to San Jacinto, 13; encamps at battlesite, 14; orders Delgado to engage Texans, 14-15; exposes self in grandstand play, 14; spends two-hour lull with Emily, 15-16; resumes hostilities on April 20, 16-17; recognizes superiority over Houston, 19; reinforced by General Cos, 19-20; orders rest for reinforcements, 19; settles down to comfort of marquee, 20; parties with Emily, 22; escapes from battlefield, 30-31; evidence of revelry, 31; capture of, 31-33; quoted, 32-33; surrenders to Houston, 34; price paid for Emily's favors, 38-39; Yellow Rose song related to in books, 51; legend concerning background, 99-111 *passim*
Satanistas: 11, 24, 29
Saracen: ridden by Houston at San Jacinto, 22
Saunders, Bull: see Santa Anna Legend, The, 99-111 *passim*
Saunders, Nathaniel and Pattie: see Santa Anna Legend, The, as cited
Saunders, Dr. Reuben: 109; see also Santa Anna Legend, The
Schirmer, G. Inc. of New York: 67
Scotch highlanders: 6
servants: indentured, 6, 9

Sherman, Colonel Sidney: reconnoiters at New Washington, 11; and Houston, 16, 20; skirmishes for Mexican cannon, 16-18; acclaimed hero in camp, 18; originates battle cry, 23; and Kentucky Volunteers, 106-107
Shiloh, Battle of: 115
slaves: prohibition of, in Texas, 6; see also servants
Smith, Deaf: 20, 22, 25, 35
soldaderas: 12, 21
songs: folksongs, art, and popular songs, 1-4 *passim*; "Song of the Texas Ranger," 53; "Songs of The Hills and Range," 85; see also listings under music at San Jacinto and Yellow Rose
Sonnichsen, Dr. C. L.: see Introduction, vii
Sons of the Knights of the Yellow Rose of Texas: 39
South: 35, 114, 115
Southwest: country of, 102; Literature of, xiv
Spain: royalist army of, 7
Spotsylvania County, Virginia: 99
statistics of Battle of San Jacinto: 29-30
Storm King mountains: 102
Swartwout, Samuel: recipient of marquee, 36
Sylvester, Sergeant James Austin: 32, 33

Tampico: 37, 104
Tennessee: 54
Texans: 14, 15, 18, 19, 22, 23, 105
Texas: xiv, 6, 7, 13, 16, 44, 105; refugees, 5; army, 12, 14, 35, 107; A&M University, xiii; centennial, 67, 68; folklore, 37; government officials, 5, 8, 9, 35; history, xii, 36; independence, viii, 25, 39, 113; Republic of, 39, 41, 105; Texas Western Press, xiii; State Library of, 52; longhorn, 93
Thompson, Private Charles: 32

135

Trinity River: 10
Turner, yellow boy: capture of, 9; warns Houston of Santa Anna's approach, 10; misleads Santa Anna, 10
Twin Sisters: see cannon

Union troops: 54
United States: 54, 104; government, 105-106, 110
University of Texas at Austin, The: 41, 52; library, 55, 65, 78
University of Texas at El Paso: xiii
Urriza, Fernandez: 15

Velasco: 41
Velasco: treaties of, 34
Veracruz: 104
Vermillion, Private Joseph: 32
Victory Song Book for Soldiers, Sailors and Marines: 79
Vince, Allen: 30
Vince ranch: 32, 33
Vince's Bayou: 23
Vince's bridge: 20, 21, 22, 23

Waring, John U.: 110
Washington, D.C.: 34, 77, 105, 106, 115
Wells, Major Lysander: 18
West, Emily D.: see Morgan, Emily
West Point, United States Military Academy of: see Santa Anna Legend, The
Wharton, John W.: 34
"Will You Come to The Bower?": 45; see also music at San Jacinto
World War I: 103
World War II: "Yellow Rose of Texas, The" in, 79-83 *passim*

Yarborough, former Senator Ralph W.: 3, 52
"Yellow Rose of Texas, The" (girl): see Morgan, Emily
"Yellow Rose of Texas, The" (song:) popularity of the song and the symbol, xii-xv *passim*; transcends national boundaries, 82; origin of, 2-4; early title, "Emily, the Maid of Morgan's Point, 45; inspired by Emily Morgan, xii, 45, 95; manuscript copy of, 41-47; text of manuscript copy, 46-47; first copyright edition of, 49-52; a Civil War marching song, 53-55 *passim*; and Republic of Texas, 44; octavo edition of 1906, 55-64; transcript variant of 1930, 65-67 *passim*; transcriptions by David W. Guion, 67-68; musical score, 69-77, 77-78; in World War II, as cited above; reprint of first edition, 85-86; Mitch Miller adaptation, the, 87-92; cover and chorus of Don George arrangement, 88, 89; boogie woogie transcription of 1956, 93-95 *passim*; predictions for the future, 95; mentioned, 45, 46, 51, 52, 53; German translation, 63
Yellow Rose Medallion, The: viii
Young, Maud Jeannie Fuller: 53
Yucatán: 104

Zacatecans: 8, 104
Zacatecas: 8
Zavala, Vice President Lorenzo de: 6, 35
Zavala, young Lorenzo de: 16, 34